P9-EJZ-839

A MIDNIGHT CLEAR

SAM HOOKER ✕ ALCY LEYVA
LAURA MORRISON
CASSONDRA WINDWALKER
DALENA STORM ✕ SEVEN JANE

WITHDRAWN

This Book is sold subject to the condition that it shall not, by way of trade or otherwise, be lent, re-sold, duplicated, hired out, or otherwise circulated without the publisher's prior written consent in any form of binding or cover other than that in which it is published and without similar condition including this condition being imposed on the subsequent purchaser.

ISBN (print): 978-1-7335994-4-3
ISBN (ebook): 978-1-7335994-5-0

Cover design by Najla Qamber
Edited by Lindy Ryan
Interior design layout by Rebecca Poole

Black Spot Books
All rights reserved.
Release date 11/5/19

This is a work of fiction. All characters and events portrayed in this novel are fictitious and are products of the author's imagination and any resemblance to actual events, or locales or persons, living or dead are entirely coincidental.

DEDICATION

To my family, who constantly remind me not to spoil my stories by telling people that everyone dies in the end. Oh, shoot.
- Sam Hooker

To those we remember. May we never forget.
- Alcy Leyva

To my mom and dad.
- Laura Morrison

To the staff of the Roanoke Review, the literary magazine who first took a chance on Sam and Dani. All any of us need is just one reader.
- Cassondra Windwalker

For Athena.
- Dalena Storm

For the only two people I would rather stay home with.
- Seven Jane

CONTENTS

THE DAUNTLESS
Sam Hooker

NEXT ... D-DOCKET..." POUNDCAKE PAUSED. HIS TONGUE lolled from the side of his mouth as he stared at the clipboard. Stared daggers at it. His bitter squint leveled threats at the page, promising grievous injury if it didn't surrender its secrets.

Snickerdoodle forced a placid smile across her face, behind which her frustration roiled. The big oaf had said the word "docket" countless times over the years. He should have accidentally memorized it by now. He couldn't be wilfully resisting it, could he?

Poundcake hadn't been appointed bailiff for his prowess in literacy. At two feet, eleven inches tall, he was by far the biggest elf in the North Pole. It made sense to everyone else that the big guy would be the bailiff, so Snickerdoodle supposed that was good enough. Of course, had anyone asked her, she'd have suggested someone with a firm grasp of the entire alphabet.

"The ... N-North ... Pole ... verse ... vuss..."

"Versus," offered Judge Fuzzybean, with as much patience as he could muster. He always had to help Poundcake with that one.

"Yeah, that. Um, *vuzzes* ... S-Sprinkles."

"The North Pole seeks the maximum penalty available," said Sugarsnap, over-enunciating the way people do when they want to seem smarter than they are.

"Of course it does," sighed the judge. "May we please hear the charges first, if that's all right with the prosecution?"

"Cookie sneakery in the first degree!" shouted Sugarsnap, shaking a manila folder above his head.

"Hey," moaned Poundcake, "I get to read those!"

"You take too long," grumbled Sugarsnap, giving an agitated wave toward the bailiff's hurt expression.

"First degree?" Sprinkles' lower lip quivered. "It was only one extra cookie!"

"Objection, Your Honor," said Snickerdoodle. "The prosecution has been reminded many times that there are no degrees of cookie sneakery."

"Sustained," the judge replied. "How does the defendant plead?"

"Naughty, Your Honor," Snickerdoodle replied as gently as she could. Sprinkles was on the verge of tears. Snickerdoodle saw in her file that she'd never been in trouble before. She cared about her clients and didn't like to see them tied up in anxious knots.

Sugarsnap, on the other hand, lived for that sort of thing. He'd gone to law school because he wanted to punish people for a living.

"Very well," said Judge Fuzzybean, not looking up from the papers in front of him. "Given that this is your first offense and you came clean about it, the court orders you to pay a fine of one poem about cookies."

Sprinkles' eyes lit up.

"A *new* poem about cookies, that is."

Sprinkles grinned. She was practically famous in openmic poetry slam circles for her odes to cookies. If Fuzzybean hadn't been a slam poet himself, Sprinkles might have gotten away with paying her debt with existing work. But no matter. She was a legend. Snickerdoodle had no doubt that she'd have something drafted before the day was out.

Judge Fuzzybean banged his gavel. Sugarsnap glared at Snickerdoodle, and she smiled back. She didn't like Sugarsnap. He was a meanie. She'd never use that kind of language out loud, but it was true. He was a real *meanie*. Genetic elfish optimism demanded that she assume he was a nice guy deep down, but Snickerdoodle had never seen any proof. She'd only seen him being a big … well, she wasn't about to swear three times in the same thought process.

It had been a light day in Candy Court. Then again, they always were. Elves never got into real trouble, much to Sugarsnap's chagrin. Before Sprinkles, the day's dockets had included a barista who'd played fast-and-loose with the standard marshmallows-to-cocoa ratio. She'd been sentenced to three afternoons of sleigh bell jingling in the snow angel garden. The docket before that had been a Failure to Whistle While Working case that got dismissed. Sugarsnap had pushed for five years of shoes without curled toes, but Snickerdoodle had proven–beyond a shadow of a doubt–that Candyfloss had been on a mandatory giggle break at the time.

"Just you try whistling and giggling at the same time," Snickerdoodle had said to the court. "It would be delightful, no doubt. But it simply isn't possible."

One docket left, Snickerdoodle thought to herself as she looked at the lone folder on the judge's bench. It was significantly thicker than average, which was exciting. It usually meant that some new carols would be entered into evidence, and the whole Candy Court would get to sing them.

"N-next … doggy…" stammered Poundcake.

"Oh, for *cinnamon swirlies*," groaned Sugarsnap.

"Objection!"

"Sustained! You'll watch your mouth in my court, counselor."

"Sorry," Sugarsnap sneered. From the way he rolled his eyes, Snickerdoodle got the impression that he wasn't sorry at all.

"N-North ... Pole..."

"Versus."

"*Fizzy* ... Gum ... Gumdrop."

"What's the charge?"

"The ... r-really ... delivery ... m-murders."

"Thank you, Bailiff," said Judge Fuzzybean. "And how does the–wait, what?"

Fuzzybean, Sugarsnap, and Snickerdoodle all stared down at their copies of the file to see what word Poundcake had mistaken for "murders," only to find that that wasn't the one he'd gotten wrong. The name of the case was "The R'lyeh Delivery Murders." For once, no one questioned how Poundcake had misread a word. Snickerdoodle couldn't begin to guess how one would pronounce "R'lyeh."

Before she could ask for clarification, a blood-curdling scream ripped through the courtroom from just beyond the bailiff's door.

"What was that?" gasped Fuzzybean.

"I think it was Gumdrop," said Poundcake.

"My client?" This was a lot for Snickerdoodle to take in. Why was he screaming? What was delivered to R'lyeh–however that was pronounced–and was it too much to hope that it was several bowls of ice cream that had been murdered?

"Wait a minute," said Fuzzybean, "Gumdrop's not even in here! Bailiff, please escort the defendant to his seat."

"All right," Poundcake warbled in a foreboding sort of sing-songy "you're not going to like it" way.

A pleasant disposition goes a long way in all facets of elf-ish life, and staying off the Naughty List was a big motivator.

To that end, most defendants opted to skip from Poundcake's door to their seats. A few have tried whistling as well, though Fuzzybean frowns on that. He says whistlers don't take Candy Court seriously enough.

Gumdrop didn't whistle. He didn't skip. He didn't even wear a happy-and-you-know-it grin. His arms were all bound up in an odd shirt with belts on. Snickerdoodle had never seen anything like it.

But that wasn't the worst part. It was his eyes. Where elves almost always have a gleam or a twinkle, Gumdrop's gaze was bleak, teetering on the edge of fear. Lack of sleep had weathered his face, his once ruddy complexion now pale and wan. He shuffled listlessly as Poundcake guided him to his chair.

Snickerdoodle was having trouble grasping the enormity of the case. "I'd like to request a recess, Your Honor."

"Recess is after lunch," said Fuzzybean.

"No, I mean I need a moment to confer with my client."

"Objection!" Sugarsnap spat.

"On what grounds?"

"Well," Sugarsnap began, searching for the words to explain what he'd thought obvious, "it's highly irregular!"

"It's a highly irregular case," Snickerdoodle replied.

"I agree," Sugarsnap retorted, "all the reason to avoid adding any more irregularity."

"Sustained."

"But Your Honor, I've never–"

"None of us have ever tried a *murder*, counselor," said Fuzzybean, whispering the frightful word. "Let's stick to what we know, shall we?"

Snickerdoodle was speechless. At her core, she was a holly jolly elf who wanted nothing more than to get along with everyone, smile, drink cocoa, and have a snowball fight that ended in giggle fits. But this didn't sit well with her. Some rugged individualist within her thought what Fuzzybean said was a load of coal, and wanted no part of it.

But elves didn't do rugged individualism. It wasn't a rule or anything, it just didn't occur to them. That made Snicker-doodle uncomfortable. She'd never asked for individualism to go occurring, all willy-nilly, in her head. She made a mental note to be on the lookout for any more wanton occurrences.

Fuzzybean moved on to reading the charges. Gumdrop was one of six elves assigned to deliver Christmas to a place called R'lyeh—no one could agree on a proper pronunciation—while Santa was delivering it to the rest of the world. They'd departed in a submarine called the Dauntless at the beginning of December, and when the craft returned at the end of January, Gumdrop was the only member of the crew still alive. He was festooned in the entrails of his comrades, surrounded by their bloody corpses. All of them bore the same wide-eyed visages of terror as Gumdrop, though they weren't shrieking like mad.

"He was screaming something over and over when they pulled him out of the Dauntless," said Fuzzybean as he rifled through the papers in front of him. "Can anyone find the transcription?"

"Iä! Iä! Cthulhu fhtagn!" Gumdrop screeched in a disturbing warble. "Ph'nglui mglw'nafh Cthulhu R'lyeh wgah'nagl fhtagn!"

"That's the one," said Fuzzybean. "And I suppose that clears up the pronunciation of R'lyeh. The court will hear opening arguments from the prosecution."

Sugarsnap glared smugly around the room as he stood. He was always eager for a win. His chronic competitiveness had made him Toymaker of the Month for seven months of the past year, three consecutive.

"May it please the court," he began, "this is an open-and-shut case. If Gumdrop wasn't guilty of murdering the rest of his crew, why wouldn't he say so? The only conclusion that might be reached through advanced interrogation techniques would be that his semblance of insanity is a ruse. A distraction. One that prevents him from having to answer a direct question with a lie. 'Did you murder the crew of the Dauntless?' Why won't he answer the question? Because lying will land him on the Naughty List, and the truth will result in a death sentence. Thank you."

Snickerdoodle scribbled furiously on a notepad as Sugarsnap took his seat. The prosecutor had a priggish look on his face, as though he'd won the case already while juggling pies to a standing ovation.

"Does the defense have an opening statement?" asked Fuzzybean, implying that Snickerdoodle should stop scribbling and start talking if she wanted to make one.

"Yes, Your Honor," Snickerdoodle replied. She took a deep breath and let it out slowly as she smoothed the front of her dress. It jingled like crazy for all the bells sewn onto it.

"As Your Honor has pointed out," she said, "this is a highly irregular case. Even the premise raises more questions than it answers. For instance, Santa has always performed all of the Christmas deliveries himself. For centuries, he and the reindeer have made the rounds unassisted. The entire world in one night. Why send elves on this delivery in particular?

"And then there's this … R'lyeh," she continued, still not sure she was getting the inflection just right. "According to the notes in the docket it's in the middle of the ocean, but according to the map, there's nothing there! Why send a submarine to the middle of the ocean?

"The prosecution's argument is absurd." She leveled a baleful look at Sugarsnap. He returned it with interest. "My client hasn't admitted guilt, and he's obviously not well enough to proclaim his innocence either. Sugarsnap doesn't know anything about advanced interrogation techniques. None of us do! What *are* advanced interrogation techniques?"

Snickerdoodle paused for effect. It was a gamble, but it paid off. Sugarsnap had no reply, other than folding his arms in a huff.

"The cause of the tragedy aboard the Dauntless is yet unknown," Snickerdoodle continued, "and no definitive evidence proves my client is at fault, intentionally or otherwise. And what does the defense mean, 'death sentence?' I don't think the Peanut Butter Penal Code even has a definition for murder. The most severe punishment I've ever seen it recommend is six months with artificial sweeteners!"

Everyone in the court gasped. Snickerdoodle was loath to bring up the case of the Christmas Carol Swearer, but under the circumstances, she felt the shock was warranted.

"Right," said Fuzzybean, drawing the word out. "Does the Peanut Butter Penal Code say anything about elves who are a potential danger to themselves or others?"

"I don't think so," said Sugarsnap. "In the south, they do prison for that sort of thing."

Gumdrop whimpered.

"Prison!" Snickerdoodle gasped. "We don't even have one of those!"

"She's right," said Fuzzybean. "I'll bet Creampuff could design one in a jiffy, though. She's a great architect."

"What?" Things were taking a weird turn. Had they

really leapt over debating guilt and landed in prison design contracts?

"He can stay in his own home until it's built," said Sugarsnap. "Under supervision, of course."

"Of course."

"Hang on–"

"Well then," said Fuzzybean, his gavel rising to strike, "if there's nothing else, the court remands–"

"Objection!"

Another gasp erupted from the court. It was turning out to be a shocking sort of day.

"You don't get to object at the sentencing!"

"With all due respect, Your Honor, when did we move from the trial to the sentencing? We've just done opening remarks!"

"Well, yes," said Fuzzybean, "it's just that ... well, cases are usually done by now. Don't you want to go to lunch?"

"Of course I do," said Snickerdoodle, "I love lunch. But my client deserves a complete trial!"

"I suppose so," Fuzzybean sighed. "How does the defendant plead?"

Snickerdoodle looked at Gumdrop. She couldn't say for sure whether his wide-eyed, vacant stare was a yearning for justice or the desperate terror of an elf drowning in madness. Either way, she knew lunch would have to wait.

"Not naughty, Your Honor."

"And just what is the point of that?" demanded Sugarsnap. "Look at him! He's as daffy as a fairy trapped in a sugar bowl! What are we supposed to do with him if he's found nice?"

"Probably the same thing we'd do if he's found naughty," agreed Fuzzybean. "He's a danger to himself and others. He'll have to be locked up."

"Perhaps," said Snickerdoodle, "but he'll be *nice*."

"Does that really matter?" Sugarsnap sneered.

"If it doesn't," said Snickerdoodle, "then we may as well convert Candy Court to a prison, because it's certainly not being used for justice."

IT WAS LATE. SNICKERDOODLE WAS TIRED, BUT SHE DIDN'T DARE sleep. Gumdrop's trial would reconvene in three days, so she didn't have long to prove his innocence.

Due to the unusual nature of the case, she'd been given time away from her toymaking *and* legal duties so that she could devote her full attention to the case. While that was good on the one hand, on the other it was bizarre. An elf without a pair of jobs? Every instinct within her was screaming at her to go out into the world and find something that needed doing. Sure, she was doing this, but what was she supposed to be thinking about in the back of her mind? Was she to devote her full attention to just one thing? Well, she supposed that she was. She just wasn't sure how that was supposed to work.

Sugarsnap had been offered the same, but he declined. He either had a harder time defying his instincts, or he was so arrogant that he felt he didn't need the time to prepare. Either was just as easy to believe.

She'd been combing through old court dockets for hours, looking for precedents. She only managed to prove to herself that the Christmas Carol Swearer was, in fact, the most heinous case ever tried in Candy Court. That one had lasted nearly an hour, and most of that was deliberation over the sentencing. What's a fitting punishment for shouting the one that starts with "G" and severely affronts the victim's apple-bobbing skills?

Mass murder! At the North Pole! This was beyond the pale. Snickerdoodle was counting on finding something approaching a precedent, and she didn't know what to do next without one. She closed her books and started baking a cake.

She needed to talk to Gumdrop, and you didn't visit the home of another elf without bringing treats. Time was running out, but she wasn't about to turn her back on centuries of elfish tradition for the sake of expediency. That was a sure-fire way to get yourself on the Naughty List.

She needed to *try* and talk to him, anyway. Whimpers and screams were all she'd heard from him thus far.

Fortunately, Snickerdoodle was an excellent baker, and she left her house with a perfectly frosted cake a mere two hours later. She wore a gleeful smile as she walked through the streets of Santa's Village. She didn't feel particularly jolly given the circumstances, but she'd have gotten weird looks had her expression been dour. Passers-by would have stopped her for obligatory hugs, and she didn't have that kind of time. It was an odd feeling, forcing a smile. She'd probably not have been surprised to learn that she was the first elf to walk past the Sleighbell Street Carollers without a genuine ear-to-ear grin.

"Hi, Snickerdoodle," said Poundcake, who for some reason was resting his dimwitted bulk against the wall beside Gumdrop's front door. "Sorry, Gumdrop's not to have any visitors."

"I'm not a visitor," said Snickerdoodle, "I'm Gumdrop's attorney. Do you remember? From Candy Court, earlier today?"

"Oh, I remember," Poundcake hastened to agree, excited to be in the know for once. "Is that for me then?"

"No, it's for Gumdrop. I'd have baked you something too, I just didn't know you'd be here. Sorry."

"Oh," said Poundcake. "That's all right. You still can't see him, though."

"What? Of course, I can. I'm his attorney!"

Poundcake's expression twisted into the sort of discomfort usually experienced as a result of having taken "all you can eat" as a challenge.

"It's just that Judge Fuzzybean said no visitors."

"I'm not a visitor."

"You brought a cake."

"That's just what you do," said Snickerdoodle, fearing her cheerful demeanor might falter under the joint assault that her stress and Poundcake's insipidness seemed to have coordinated. "Look, I'm sure that Judge Fuzzybean wouldn't object to Gumdrop meeting with his attorney."

"He would, actually," came a voice from behind her. She knew who it was without having to turn around, though she did that anyway. Hard to glare at someone standing behind you.

"Sugarsnap," Snickerdoodle spat. At least she could give her smiling muscles a rest.

"Snickerdoodle," the prosecutor replied in a gloating, if not condescending, tone. "I met with Fuzzybean in his chambers after you left the courtroom so hastily. He agreed that this case was complicated enough without the defendant having secret meetings."

"Secret meetings? I'm his attorney!" She'd had to declare that often enough in the last minute that she was starting to doubt it was true.

"And I'm his prosecutor," Sugarsnap smirked, "but you don't see me having secret meetings with him, do you?"

"No, but you–" Snickerdoodle shut her eyes and shook her head. "That's irrelevant! It's perfectly normal for people accused of crimes to consult with their attorneys."

"There's nothing *normal* about this case. That's the point. We don't *normally* talk to defendants outside the courtroom."

"We don't *normally* have defendants accused of mass murder either. Special cases require special measures."

"That's where I disagree," said Sugarsnap, rocking on his heels. "And unfortunately for you, Judge Fuzzybean agrees with me."

"It's true," said Poundcake, at once excited to have something to contribute to the conversation and uncomfortable doing so. "Fuzzybean says I can't let you in." His enthusiasm abated slightly as his brain caught up. "Sorry," he added weakly.

"It's fine," Snickerdoodle sighed, though it most certainly wasn't. The law was complicated. That's the whole reason there were lawyers in the first place. Gumdrop barely had a grasp on reality at the moment, much less the capacity to speak for himself in Candy Court! While it might have been argued he was as sane as anyone who'd made it through law school, you'd need a lawyer to argue that for you, and they're expensive.

Having seen that she wasn't going to get past Poundcake before talking to the judge, Snickerdoodle left.

SNICKERDOODLE SLEPT FITFULLY THAT NIGHT, FALLING WELL short of the full hour of sleep recommended by the Elfish Health Council. She forced a smile as she waited on the bench outside Fuzzybean's chambers, contenting herself with the fact that she didn't have it as bad as Gumdrop, who looked as though he hadn't slept in a month. She didn't like taking solace in the misfortune of others, but the elfish optimism gene causes silver linings to take root in some pretty dark places.

Fuzzybean rounded the corner, stopping in his tracks when he saw Snickerdoodle. His eyes narrowed as if he expected her to try and sell him something.

"Snickerdoodle." He greeted her warily and tried to hurry past her into his office.

"Judge Fuzzybean!" Snickerdoodle leapt from the bench. She was practically shaking with litigious fury as she followed the judge through the door. "I need to talk to you about my access to my client! I know this is an unusual case, but I should have been given a chance to weigh in on–"

"Yes, yes," Fuzzybean flailed his hands in irritation, as though fending off her assault with amateur martial arts. "Get to the point, Snickerdoodle! I've got three dockets today, not to mention an increased quota of jack-in-the-box ... es ... jacks-in-the-box? Boxes?" He shook his head. "I've got toys to build! Now, spit it out!"

"I demand to be allowed to speak to my client!"

"What's stopping you?"

Snickerdoodle balked. "I thought you were."

Fuzzybean gave her a look that could have curdled cement. "Even if I wanted to forbid you to speak to Gumdrop for some ridiculous reason I'd think twice, maybe three times, about how much I'd want to avoid this exact conversation."

"But Sugarsnap said ... and Poundcake..."

"Let me guess," sighed Fuzzybean, "Sugarsnap told a fib to keep you away from Gumdrop? And Poundcake went along with it?"

"Well, if you didn't–"

"I wish I could say that I expected more from Poundcake, but he's not the brightest light on the string."

Snickerdoodle balked. Sugarsnap *lied?* The nerve! The gall! Did he not understand the veracity of the Naughty List?

To be fair, Snickerdoodle had never actually seen the consequences of being on it, but she had no desire to find out.

"Close your door on the way out," said Fuzzybean. He was reading over some papers on his desk, no longer looking at her.

"Th-thank you, Your Honor," she stammered as she left. Fuzzybean shot a grumpy mumble at her back, leading her to wonder whether that was whence the word "grumble" came.

Snickerdoodle walked as quickly as she could back to Gumdrop's house. She rehearsed an apology for not having a treat with her. She nearly ran home to bake one, but she'd rather avoid Sugarsnap and Poundcake, and they'd only be in court for three dockets. She avoided looking herself in her mind's eye, not wanting to deal with the disapproving look she was sure to find there. It wasn't particularly brave of her, was it?

Unfortunately, Gumdrop wasn't home. Or, at least, no one answered the door, and there were no lights visible through the windows. Where could he have gone? Or, if he was there, why didn't he answer the door?

Snickerdoodle sighed. At least she hadn't actually committed a pastry-related *faux pas*.

Certain things aren't supposed to happen. Traffic lights never turn blue, despite the predictions of classic rock songs. Pigs prefer to remain firmly on the ground, moss does not gather on stones in motion, and elves are never at a loss for what to do next.

Snickerdoodle had never "played it by ear." She'd never "winged it." There was a rhythm to her life, a logical flow from one task to the next. A scientist might wonder whether it was a cultural phenomenon or a genetic one. However, once they realized how much magic was at work with elfish physiology, they'd probably gone out for sandwiches instead. Scientists don't truck with magic, and they love sandwiches.

Someone was covering Snickerdoodle's toy quotas. Someone else was speaking up for defendants in Candy Court. No one was answering Gumdrop's door. She just didn't know what to do next.

Panic started to rise in Snickerdoodle's chest. Her heart thundered in her ears and stars swam in her vision. She needed something to do, and she needed it fast.

The Dauntless! Had anyone investigated the gory scene of the alleged crime? There was another chilling thought. Most elves had never seen a movie with a dead person in it unless the ghosts of Christmases Past, Present, and Future fit the bill. To go into a metal casement that had served as a tomb for several of her kin?

But it had to be done. Thankful for a purpose for the present moment, Snickerdoodle started walking toward the docks. It occurred to her, as she stopped at a roasted chestnut vendor for the very reason one would assume, that Gumdrop didn't seem to have spoken a word since he returned from that fateful voyage. If no one had cleaned out the submarine, it might be able to tell her more than that unfortunate survivor.

A dense layer of frost covered the hull of the half-submerged craft. It bobbed lazily in the seawater beside the dock, occasionally giving a hollow "gong" sound as the waves pushed it against its moorings.

"You're not supposed to be over there," came a voice from behind her.

"I've been getting that a lot."

"That doesn't make it any less true," said the dockmaster. It took Snickerdoodle a moment to recognize Smitty. He didn't wear a sailor's cap and coat on the factory floor, but he worked near her station during his toy shift. He was a tricycle assemblyman, and a fine one at that, if the *Honorable Mentions* section of last quarter's employee newsletter were any indication.

"I'm representing the survivor," Snickerdoodle explained. "His name is Gumdrop."

Smitty sighed and stared at the rough timbers of the dock, shaking his head. "Terrible business, that. I hear he still hasn't spoken a word."

"You've heard right. I just need to see if there are any clues aboard that will help me defend him."

"Defend him?" Smitty looked as though Snickerdoodle had slapped him across the face. Or, at least, Snickerdoodle assumed that was the sort of face that would line up with face-slapping. She'd never seen it done.

"Yes," said Snickerdoodle. "I'm his attorney. That's what attorneys do."

"But he killed his comrades!"

"Allegedly."

Smitty scratched his dimpled chin in thought. He shuffled one of his feet, the bell at the end of the curled toe of his galoshes jingling as it dragged across the boards of the dock.

"Look, I know what you're thinking," Snickerdoodle said. "And you may be right. He may be guilty. But what if he's not? I'll sleep better with the verdict either way if I can honestly say I did everything I could to get to the truth."

"I can't argue with that," said Smitty. "But I'll need you to sign the dock logs first."

"Can I sign them on the way out?"

Smitty grimaced and nodded toward the Dauntless. "They haven't cleaned it out, aside from removing the ... well, you know. You can go in there if you want, but you're not spreading the muck around on my logbook. Come on, I'll loan you—er, *give* you—some boots and gloves."

Smitty was right. As luck would have it, other than the bodies of Gumdrop's fellow crewmembers, nothing had been cleaned out of the submarine. Whether that luck was good or bad could be the subject of a heated debate. Preferably not one over dinner.

There was a particular demographic served by the Stocking Stuffers division who had an affinity for gag gifts. Whoopee cushions, shock buzzers, fake vomit, that sort of thing. The ages of the demographics were peculiar: children between eight and twelve and men in their forties with children between eight and twelve. Snickerdoodle happened to be working in the building next to Stocking Stuffers on the day that an unstable prototype fart pill had an unfortunate chemical reaction when gift-wrapped with earwax-flavored jelly beans. The resulting noxious cloud lingered around the building for weeks, guaranteeing that Snickerdoodle would never forget the stench.

Until she opened the door of that submarine, she was sure she'd never smell anything that wretched ever again. But then, there she was.

The inside of the submarine was as horrifying as its smell was revolting. Bloody handprints covered the walls. Blood splatter and viscera were everywhere, and her borrowed boots squelched with every step on the gory floor.

Law school hadn't prepared her for this! Neither had the Toymakers Academy, for that matter. It seemed futile to list off everything in her life that had failed to supply her with the skills necessary to pick through the stinking mortal remains of the dead for clues as to the cause of their demise, but strangely enough, it helped. She blamed her grocer as she looked under a table. She scolded her barista as she looked over a navigational chart. She groused about her bowling team, her hairdresser, and her hugging coach. She was about to start in on Sugarsnap when she noticed a little cabinet door that wouldn't shut all the way.

She wished the statue she found in the cabinet had been an art student's garish first attempt at sculpture, but she knew in her bones that that wasn't true. It was about eight inches tall, a vaguely anthropoid figure squatting on a pedestal covered in undecipherable writing. It had long claws and narrow wings, and it appeared to have an octopus on its head. Merely looking at the thing flooded her with a cold, haunted panic. She shoved it into her knapsack and bolted from the submarine.

The best smile that she could muster in the name of keeping up appearances probably did her more harm than good. It was a tight-lipped mockery of good cheer, the rictus of a nightmare that had slithered its way into the waking world to feast on the pleasant days other pedestrians must have been having before she shuffled past them.

This is fine, she thought as she made a beeline for her house. And why wouldn't it be? Surely, the unspeakable terror in her knapsack wasn't the source of Gumdrop's madness! No harm, then, in bringing it into her home and staring at it for a while, right? Right.

That was just what she did. She cleaned the gore off the thing, set it on her coffee table, and arranged some cookies and sugarplums in front of it.

Wait, why had she done that? Snickerdoodle shook her head. Craven statues didn't get hungry, did they? She was fairly certain she hadn't just made an offering of homemade sweets to a demonic idol, but she hadn't slept well. Anything was possible.

Snickerdoodle rubbed her eyes. The lids felt heavy, as though the weight of restless aeons were pulling them down, down into fitful darkness. She sat in her coziest chair, resolving to have a look at the horrible thing for a moment while she collected her wits.

The bleak, grey horizon alone was enough to plunge her into the depths of despair, the likes of which are known to no one but teenagers as their parents use spitty thumbs to clean some smudge, unseen to anyone but them, from their faces. Her despair swept right past foreboding and sprinted toward terror as she beheld the monstrosity rising out of the vacant sea. Relentless waves lapped at the base of the impossibly tall towers, the non-Euclidian angles of their construction leaving her with doubt as to how they resisted the pull of the earth. As terrifying as the prospect of climbing the blackened stairs was, her aversion to the towers paled in comparison to the gaping maw before her, leading down, down into the bowels of the dank and fetid soil. To her shock and disgust, she relented to some morbid compulsion and found herself descending into that harrowing darkness.

Once she'd descended far enough for the light of the grey sky to disappear behind her, the whispering began. The voices were all around her, pouring poison and malice into her ears, coaxing her as a cat chatters sweetly at a bird to come down, let go, join them in the madness ... in the dark ... in eternal dreamless sleep...

Snickerdoodle awoke with a start. It was the middle of the night. She didn't know whether to breathe a sigh of relief, to scream, or to cry. She settled for making a batch of sugar cookies. That's elfish instincts for you. While they baked in the oven, she constructed a fort with every pillow in the house, using proper Euclidean right angles without exception.

The oven timer dinged. She ate the cookies in the pillow fort, washed them down with a mug of cocoa, and cocooned herself in a blanket before drifting back into what she hoped would be a pleasant, dreamless sleep.

NEVER UNDERESTIMATE THE POWER OF A PILLOW FORT, ESPECIALLY when the load-bearing cushions are buttressed by elfish magic. When Snickerdoodle emerged, she was well-rested enough to walk on sunshine. She didn't, of course, as sunshine isn't load-bearing. Unless one happens to be a pixie, and then one has other problems.

It was late in the morning, but she might have time to talk to Gumdrop unimpeded if she hurried. While a dozen cupcakes were baking, she put the grotesque statue back in her knapsack. Once the perfectly frosted cupcakes were hastily arranged in a bouquet, she hurried out the door and quickstepped her way to Gumdrop's house.

There was no one outside the door. That was a good sign. Her heart was pounding as she knocked politely on the door.

She waited. No answer came. Perhaps Gumdrop hadn't heard her? She knocked again, a bit more forcefully.

Was he even capable of answering the door? He'd barely managed walking across the courtroom last time she'd seen him. She chided herself for even thinking of opening the door and entering unannounced.

Still no answer. She knocked again, even louder, hoping that Gumdrop would answer the door.

"Come in," sang a voice from within the house. Relief

washed over her. She squared her shoulders, turned the knob, and walked into Gumdrop's darkened living room.

"Hello, Snickerdoodle," came a gloating voice from the silhouette in the rocking chair.

"Wait," she said, "is that–"

A match flared to life as Sugarsnap lit a candle on the little table beside the chair.

"Sugarsnap!" The smug look on the prosecutor's face revealed his satisfaction with Snickerdoodle's surprise. "What are you doing here? Where's Gumdrop?"

"He's in the bedroom," Sugarsnap tilted his head toward a hallway leading farther into the house. "I gave him some warm milk with a little bit of nutmeg in it. I think this is the first sleep he's had since he got back."

Was it really that bad? Snickerdoodle had seen Gumdrop's grisly expression that day in court. He definitely hadn't had much sleep, and it was altogether possible that Sugarsnap wasn't lying this time.

"What's in it for you?" she spat.

"I beg your pardon?" If Sugarsnap was feigning offense, he was a decent actor.

"You didn't help him sleep just to be nice. You're not a nice elf. Why are you helping him?"

Sugarsnap fixed Snickerdoodle with a hurt and disappointed look. He shook his head.

"Some of us care about more than this case," he said.

Snickerdoodle didn't budge. She continued her onslaught of squinty suspicion with extreme prejudice.

"Oh, all right," Sugarsnap relented, rolling his eyes. "He can't talk to you if he's asleep, and you've either grown a backbone and come in here against the rules, or you've talked to Fuzzybean. Which is it?"

Snickerdoodle continued to glare. Sugarsnap shrugged.

"It doesn't matter. Ooo, are those cupcakes?"

"They're not for you!"

"What's in your knapsack?"

Snickerdoodle froze mid-expression-of-scorn. She had no intention of sharing her hard-won evidence with the prosecution before she'd had a chance to talk with her client about it, but she was no good at deception. Deception was basically lying. Plus, sharing was her favorite.

"Oh, give it up," Snickerdoodle deflected. "You have no right to stop me from talking to Gumdrop, and I've had enough of your distractions."

Sugarsnap giggled. "All I was–"

"Furthermore," Snickerdoodle interrupted in a fit of realization, "my client has the right to have his attorney present for any questioning. So if anyone has the right to deny someone access to Gumdrop, it's me! I'm anyone, and you're someone!"

"Now, hang on just a minute–"

"You know, I don't think I will. Please leave the premises immediately. My client and I will see you in court."

Snickerdoodle opened the door and gave Sugarsnap an insistent look. His confident smile slid into a dark glare built on a solid foundation of chagrin at having been dressed down so firmly and was raising the framework of a threat.

"You'll be sorry you took that tone with me," he said, rising to his full height and bringing to bear all the intimidation that two feet, three inches afforded him. Unfortunately for him, Snickerdoodle was two-foot-four.

"Take a cupcake on your way out," said Snickerdoodle, holding the bouquet toward him.

Sugarsnap stomped out the front door in a huff. That was

two of Snickerdoodle's gambits that worked out in her favor: she finally had sole access to her client, and the prosecutor didn't get any cupcakes that weren't intended for him. She'd guessed that he would resist doing what she told him to do, and she was right.

The downside to having been right was that she was now alone in Gumdrop's house. Well, not quite alone. It was actually slightly worse than that. It occurred to Snickerdoodle that she had no idea how Gumdrop might react to … well, *anything*. She didn't know if he was guilty of mass murder. She didn't even know if he understood anything that was happening. Was he the one who'd hidden the grotesque statue in the little cabinet on the submarine? What would he do if he knew that Snickerdoodle had it? Was it safe for her to be alone with him?

That was the most worrisome of all of the questions swirling around in her head, and not just because of the immediate danger. Like all elves, the closest thing to fear she'd ever experienced was a healthy respect for toymaking machinery. You could get a severe bump on the noggin if you got too close to a toy train track bender. But it had never occurred to her that she should have a reason to fear for her safety at the hands of another elf.

She heard a yelp and a whimper from down the hallway. Gumdrop could wake up at any time! She could be in real danger!

Snickerdoodle made great haste in arranging the cupcake bouquet on the dining table. Her calligraphy wasn't up to her standard on the thoughtful "get well soon" note she left with them, but it would have to do. She bolted from the house without any further ado.

She didn't know what to do next. She wandered the

streets of Santa's Village for a while, eventually taking a seat on a bench facing the frozen pond in Poinsettia Park. She watched some penguins slide around on their tummies and took stock of the situation.

She had to be in court tomorrow. She could finally talk to her client, but she didn't know if he could respond, or if he might try to ... you know. She didn't know the details of the events in question. No one did. There were no witnesses, no precedents, and no prison if he was found guilty. What was she to do?

Snickerdoodle had never had so many questions and so few answers in her life. There was only one person who could help her now.

"I REALLY THOUGHT SOMEONE WOULD HAVE COME TO ME LONG before now," said Santa.

"I didn't know what else to do," Snickerdoodle replied. She stared down at the marshmallows in her cocoa, torn between wanting to curl into a ball of anxiety over the case and collapsing in a giggle fit about the fact that she was there. *There.* Sitting on the hearth, having a mug of cocoa and a one-on-one chat with The Man Himself, in his own house! This was a once-in-a-lifetime opportunity for most elves. Well, anyone who wasn't an executive, or Senior Toy Designer at least. She just wished that it hadn't taken something so awful for her to have a reason to knock on Santa's door.

"I didn't expect that you would," Santa said. "I never wanted to put Gumdrop through Candy Court at all, given the circumstances. But the Holly Jolly Justice Council insisted."

They sat in silence for a moment. Snickerdoodle had so many questions, she hardly knew where to begin.

"You're probably wondering why," said Santa, as though he were able to read her mind. Then again, she didn't know that he couldn't. For want of a more cogent reply, she merely nodded.

Santa sighed. "There's no easy answer to that, I'm afraid. How much do you know about the nature of good and evil?"

Snickerdoodle's brow wrinkled in confusion. Of all the topics she hadn't been prepared to discuss with Santa, that was ... one of them.

"I know about the Naughty and Nice Lists," she ventured.

"All right," Santa nodded, "we can start there. People do naughty and nice things all year long, and the balance of their deeds puts their names on one list or the other. Nice derives from good, but it's ... well, it's *removed*. If you think of pure goodness as the raging inferno at the core of the sun, *nice* is like warming up a bit by standing in a sunbeam on a cold day."

"And naughty," said Snickerdoodle, "derives from evil?"

"Oh, heavens no," said Santa. "Well, yes. Sometimes. It depends." He drew in a breath in preparation to speak, then paused, exhaled, and cast a consternated gaze up at the ceiling.

"Well, there's the intent," he said eventually. "The children who end up on the Naughty List aren't there because they're evil. Most of the time, they're just misguided, or too curious about things like the effects of paint on sofas that aren't for sitting. That sort of mischief. That's why we did away with the whole coal-in-the-stocking thing."

"Naughty and nice ... both derive from good, then?"

"That tends to be the case," Santa said slowly, choosing his words with care. "That's not to say that there aren't evil things on the Naughty List."

"Evil *people*, you mean."

"In most cases, yes."

To Snickerdoodle's credit, Santa was only blowing her mind a bit. Elfish instincts were so firmly rooted in niceness that more primal concepts like good and evil didn't apply to them.

"Good and evil need each other to exist," Santa continued. "There's a spectrum between them, and that spectrum is a dimension of the universe. Without that dimension, certain aspects of existence would close in on themselves. Anything that previously aligned along that now-non-existent dimension would … well, they'd stop working right. It's hard to explain."

"It would be like the Naughty and Nice Lists getting shuffled together."

Santa fixed Snickerdoodle with a look of incredulous pride.

"Maybe it's not that hard after all," mumbled Snickerdoodle, turning bright red.

"Don't sell yourself short," Santa said through a grin. "Anyway, the forces of good and evil talk about eradicating each other all the time, but it would be bad if either of them ever managed it. Luckily for the universe, it's essentially impossible. Still, just to make sure the balance is maintained, the universe evolved the concept of justice."

"Oh, I know about justice," said Snickerdoodle, perking up at the conversation's turn toward the familiar. "That's why I'm here, after all. To get justice for Gumdrop."

Santa adopted a pensive expression and stared thoughtfully at the ceiling for a moment.

"It's a lot like that, yes," he said after a while. "But what I'm talking about is much older, much more primal. Tell me, Snickerdoodle … do you know the meaning of life?"

"To find one's gift," Snickerdoodle replied. "And to use it in service of a worthy purpose."

"This is why I love working with the elves," Santa smiled. "The people down south spend their whole lives trying to figure that out, and many of them never do."

"Really?" Snickerdoodle balked in disbelief. "It's simple, though. Can't we just ... I don't know, send them all letters or something?"

"It should be so easy. Unfortunately, they've all built it up to be something much more arcane and unreachable in their minds. The truth is too simple. They wouldn't believe it."

"Oh." The word sounded small. Granted, "oh" is a small word, but there was more to it than that. Snickerdoodle tried to grasp the enormity of an entire race of people stumbling around in the dark, occasionally glimpsing the switch that turned on the lights, and thinking, "nope, too easy. That couldn't be it," and stumbling elsewhere.

"Yeah," said Santa. That word was equally small, but it was everything that he could have said.

Santa reached for the cocoa pot and refilled both of their mugs. He dropped a couple of marshmallows into his, settled into his chair, and took in a thoughtful breath.

"The meaning of life," he said, slowly, thoughtfully, "for all of us here in the Village, is the service of justice. We make deliveries as the Lists demand that we should. We're part of a much larger entity of the cosmos, one which maintains the balance between good and evil. That is our greater purpose. When you follow it all the way down to the roots, the justice that we serve by fulfilling the Lists keeps the universe in balance."

"I see," said Snickerdoodle, who understood the concept, but was having trouble coming to grips with the totality of it.

"You see well enough," said Santa with a wink, apparently reading her thoughts again. That was starting to creep Snickerdoodle out.

"Occasionally, things get too far out of balance," Santa continued. "Do you remember what Gumdrop was shouting in the courtroom?"

"It was gibberish," said Snickerdoodle, not even bothering to wonder how Santa could have known about that, given that he wasn't there. She figured if he could see you when you're sleeping and know when you're awake, he'd have ways of knowing when severely disturbed elves were shouting ominous gibberish in Candy Court.

"He said *'Ph'nglui mglw'nafh Cthulhu R'lyeh wgah'nagl fhtagn!'* That means 'In his house at R'lyeh, dead Cthulhu waits dreaming.'"

There are certain things that you just don't do. Swearing in front of grandmothers is one. Nodding when something makes absolutely no sense is another. At least Snickerdoodle wasn't doing the swearing one.

"There are things older and stranger in the world than any one person will ever learn," said Santa. "I don't want to burden you with any more than you've already got to deal with, so suffice it to say that Cthulhu should never have made his way onto the Naughty List..."

"But he did."

"But he did." Santa sipped his cocoa and sighed. "The evil that sleeps beneath the sea in R'lyeh transcends the concepts of naughty and nice. It's far beyond the justice that's ours to deliver. I wish I could explain it, but that's beyond my understanding. His name was on the list, and so the coal had to be delivered. I sent six of my best and bravest to the sunken city of R'lyeh in that submarine, and ... well, you know how that ended."

"I thought we did away with the whole coal-in-the-stocking thing."

"We did, but ancient evil gets ancient justice."

Snickerdoodle nodded. "But Santa, don't you always … I mean, isn't it your job to–"

"To make the deliveries?" Santa's gruff voice dipped nearly to a whisper. "Not this time. I wish it had been me. Me alone. But the lore of universal justice was clear on the matter, and I … couldn't."

Snickerdoodle would never forget the look on Santa's face when his eyes turned up to meet hers. It was a pained, haunted gaze. The full weight of his guilt pressed down on him, the unrelenting burden of the six elves' fates were a millstone around his soul.

"Maybe I'd have been strong enough to resist the madness that befell Gumdrop. Maybe not. All I know is that their sacrifice has maintained the balance. What I don't know … was justice worth the cost?"

They sat in silence for a long time. How long, Snickerdoodle couldn't have guessed, and she didn't try. She'd sit in silence with Santa and his grief for as long as she must. That was just what you did when the people you care about are in distress.

The long silence gave her time to think, and Santa had given her plenty to think about. She knew a lot more about the cause of the horrible fates that befell all of the elves in question, as well as a glimpse into the inner workings of the universal forces of good, evil, and justice, yet she felt as though she'd barely inched toward a proper defense for her client.

But how could she do any better? She still had no way of knowing whether he'd committed murder. Perhaps he did, or perhaps he'd barely escaped victimhood himself. That either made him the most or least fortunate of the crew of the Dauntless.

They finished their cocoa, and Santa bade Snickerdoodle farewell. She'd nearly made it back to her house when the weight of the gruesome statue in her knapsack reminded her that there were still too many unanswered questions. She still wasn't entirely sure that she'd be safe, but she had to try talking to Gumdrop again. She didn't know what she hoped to learn, exactly. She was prepared for the possibility that he might be guilty. There was an excellent chance that the architectural firms of Santa's Village would soon be bidding on a prison design contract. One that Cookiedough, Eggnog & Snowangel was likely to win.

It didn't matter. She forced herself not to hope that Gumdrop was innocent. She wanted him to be, but wanting wasn't enough. She needed to know, and she didn't want compassion to sway her objectivity. Gumdrop clearly wasn't well, and he might never be again. Perhaps prison would be the best place for him?

It didn't matter. No matter what verdict Fuzzybean handed down, Snickerdoodle needed to know the truth. Whether Gumdrop went free or spent the rest of his life behind bars, she had to know that she'd done everything in her power to find the truth. Elves lived a very, very long time. They assumed that it was forever, but no one had gotten that far yet. Either way, it was a very long time for her to be haunted by the wrong decision.

Snickerdoodle let herself in without knocking. That was clever. She hadn't technically given him the cupcakes the last time she came to visit, and since she wasn't invited in, she technically wasn't visiting now. The moment of smug satisfaction she'd intended to allow herself was cut short by a high-pitched whimper. One that sounded like it was considering a new career as a giggle. The hairs rose on the back of her neck and insisted that she bolt for the door right this instant, or there would be no dessert for a month, young lady!

She wouldn't give in to fear. She left her knapsack on the table and crept into the hallway.

"Gumdrop?"

The whimper-cackle again. It was the nervous, desperate laughter that young people employed in response to jokes made by the fathers of their significant others.

"It's Snickerdoodle," she said, undeterred. "I'm your attorney. Do you remember me?"

If Snickerdoodle had thought it was probably too much to ask that he'd respond coherently, she'd have been right. On the bright side, Gumdrop shifted from the whimpering cackle to a glottal whine in a descending register. It wasn't the sort of thing you'd buy tickets to hear in a fancy opera hall, but if you were looking to creep out a lawyer tiptoeing through a darkened house, it was just the thing.

Snickerdoodle's pulse pounded in her ears as she reached the door to his bedroom. *Run*, demanded her sense of self-preservation. *Just get out of here! It's too bad about Gumdrop, but what's the sense in adding "it's too bad about Snickerdoodle" to that?* Fortunately, she was an elf. A very, very long lifetime of smiling and singing and gifts of baked goods had instilled a measure of resolve against things like this. Gumdrop was a good elf who'd seen some unimaginable horrors beneath the bleak and unforgiving sea. If ever any elf deserved a measure of common elfish courtesy, it was Gumdrop.

Snickerdoodle took a deep breath, let it out in a trembling sigh, and turned to enter the room.

If anything, it was anticlimactic. That was a relief, though she couldn't help feeling mildly disappointed. She'd braced herself to look into the wild, bloodshot eyes of a savage bent on flaying her alive and making a festive suit of her skin. Instead, she saw a tiny, frightful elf shrunk into a corner and hugging his knees. Sure, his fearful gaze was haunted by the terrible blackness he'd beheld in the deep, as anyone's would be under the circumstances, but he didn't unburden himself of that to Snickerdoodle. To her, he extended his pain and his sorrow at the condition of his madness. Although he couldn't hide the savage darkness within him, he was obviously doing everything in his power to keep that to himself.

Snickerdoodle sat with him awhile. It occurred to her that he probably hadn't been involved in a regular conversation in a very long time, so she talked to him about everyday life in the Village. She'd have caught him up on gossip if that were the sort of thing that elves did, but everyone knew that the road to the Naughty List was paved with barbed quips about other people's business. Instead, she told him that popcorn strings were enjoying a resurgence in popularity. She knew quite a bit about the upcoming effort to make the bells on the toes of their shoes very slightly smaller. Not only would it save on materials, but it would also move the notes they rang from a C to a C sharp, which the marketing department agreed was more in keeping with Christmas cheer.

As she went on at length about her favorite new paper snowflake techniques, she noticed that Gumdrop had stopped whimpering. He hadn't stopped shivering or hugging his knees, nor had he returned to the standard elfish practice of unwavering eye contact, but it was progress nonetheless.

"You're not a monster," she declared. "Twist my tinsel, there's no way you're guilty! If anything, you're the least fortunate victim of this whole fiasco. Now, how do we prove that in Candy Court?"

That was going to take a great deal of consideration, and that wasn't going to happen without a stiff cup of cocoa. Snickerdoodle took Gumdrop by the hand and led him into the kitchen, which took a considerable amount of coaxing. Gumdrop was about as trusting of her as a plate of sugar cookies should have been, seeing as she'd skipped lunch. She put on the kettle, fired up the oven, and before long she had two mugs of cocoa and a plate of gingerbread men on the table in front of them. She considered not icing carefree smiles onto them, then chided herself for it. Yes, time was short, and yes, she was hungry; but wasn't it elfish tradition that had carried them this far? Snickerdoodle thought so. She wasn't about to turn her back on those traditions now.

Snickerdoodle worked through the night, scribbling in her notebook and helping Gumdrop take sips of cocoa now and then. It seemed to soothe his trembling a bit, but did nothing for the haunted look in his eyes. All things considered, it was a discredit to her profession that she was trying to cure him of his maladies–or at least the appearance of his maladies–before he'd had his day in court.

Luckily for Snickerdoodle, Gumdrop still trembled in terror at the memory of the sleeping god he'd beheld in distant R'lyeh while Poundcake stammered through the quotidian task of announcing the docket.

"How does the defendant plead?" asked Judge Fuzzybean.

"Not naughty," Snickerdoodle replied.

"Objection!" shouted Sugarsnap.

"I'm not going to dignify that by overruling it," said

Fuzzybean. "For the last time, defendants can plead 'not naughty' if they want."

"But look at him!" Sugarsnap gestured toward the defendant's table with all the panache of a Danish prince waxing gothic in a crypt. "He's all twitchy. You don't get twitchy like that if everything's above board!"

"Actually," said Fuzzybean, "I think he looks a bit calmer than a few days ago."

"May it please the court," said Snickerdoodle, "I'd like to enter something into evidence."

"Objection!"

"One more time," growled Fuzzybean, waggling his gavel in Sugarsnap's direction.

She reached into her knapsack and drew out the grotesque statue she'd found in the Dauntless. Gumdrop gave a mad yelp and fell to his knees.

"Iä! Iä!" Gumdrop shouted. "Cthulhu fhtagn! Ph'nglui mglw'nafh Cthulhu R'lyeh wgah'nagl fhtagn!"

"Order!" shouted Fuzzybean, banging his gavel over Gumdrop's shouting. It took a few minutes for Poundcake to remove Gumdrop from the courtroom so his trial could continue.

"What *is* that thing?" demanded Sugarsnap.

"I'm not sure, exactly," said Snickerdoodle. "I found it in the Dauntless."

"What? Why did you go in the submarine? Your Honor, she tampered with evidence!"

"No, I didn't! I collected evidence and brought it to court."

"Sounds like tampering to me."

"Hang on," said Fuzzybean, "I don't see how we can continue without the defendant in the room."

"We can," said Snickerdoodle, before Sugarsnap could

object. "Gumdrop isn't well, Your Honor, but he's not a murderer."

"How could you possibly know that?" Sugarsnap had a hand on his hip, the other gesticulating wildly above his head.

"Easy now, little teapot."

"Objection!"

Fuzzybean sighed. "Fine, I'll sustain that one. Let's refrain from name-calling."

"The prosecution demands a life sentence!" Emboldened by his tiny victory, the little teapot smelled blood in the water.

"You've hardly proven your case," Fuzzybean began.

"Oh, that's all right," said Snickerdoodle. "The defense requests a life sentence as well."

Sugarsnap opened his mouth to object out of habit, but froze and closed it again. Everyone in the courtroom stared at her.

"That's not usually the way that 'not naughty' pleas are intended to work out," Fuzzybean said slowly.

"I know, but like I said, Gumdrop isn't well."

"Don't listen to her, Your Honor! It's a trick, it has to be a trick. What's your game, Snickerdoodle?"

"It's not a game. I just want what's best for Gumdrop."

"So you admit that you have an ulterior motive."

"No, I don't! The best interests of my client are my primary motive. That's how lawyers work."

"This is highly irregular, Your Honor. I must insist that … Your Honor?"

Judge Fuzzybean didn't look well. He'd stopped listening to their argument and was transfixed by the statue.

Snickerdoodle cleared her throat. "Your Honor?"

"Iä…" Fuzzybean grunted.

"Oh, dear," Snickerdoodle swore. Fearing more elves

succumbing to Gumdrop's fate, she snatched the statue from the evidence table and shoved it into her knapsack.

"Hey," said Poundcake, "that's evidence!"

"Objection!" shouted Sugarsnap, eyes wide with manic glee.

"What?" Fuzzybean shook his head. "Hang on, I was looking at that. How am I supposed to know when great Cthulhu wakes in R'lyeh if ... wait, what?"

"Can we continue this in your chambers, Your Honor? I've had a conversation with Santa, and–"

"You talked to Santa without me?" Sugarsnap went *little teapot* again. "Your Honor, I have a series of objections that–"

"Yes, right," said Fuzzybean, standing from his chair and clearly enjoying that everyone else stood as well. "You two, in my chambers, now."

THE DELIBERATIONS IN FUZZYBEAN'S CHAMBERS SHOULDN'T HAVE taken as long as they did, but true to Sugarsnap's word, he had an impressive series of objections that needed overruling. In the end, Fuzzybean ruled that there was not sufficient evidence to convict Gumdrop of murder; however, all of them agreed that he couldn't be left to his own devices in his current state. For Snickerdoodle, this turned out to be the most challenging part of the whole ordeal. Fuzzybean was a traditionalist. He didn't truck with things like creative sentencing (or any toy that had been designed in the last hundred years, for that matter).

On top of that, Sugarsnap was out for blood. It would come to light years later that he was deep in the pockets of Big Artificial Sweetener, a lobby group with some strange ideas about convincing people that sugar was immoral, and a prison was central to their master plan. Luckily, they didn't make it very far, as artificial sweeteners are the culinary equivalent of disappointment.

In the end, the biggest problem that Snickerdoodle faced was finding two jobs that Gumdrop could manage under the burden of his madness. An outsider might question why he'd need even one job, much less two, and then be waylaid with questions like, "how dare you, sir or madam, as the case may be?" and "how did you find your way to Santa's Village?" and "would you like another cup of cocoa?"

Elves have two jobs. Grass is green, water is wet, and other mundane observations as well.

Several years later, Snickerdoodle was waiting on a moonlit pier next to Cookiepuff and Toffee. The two of them were dressed in white coats, and Cookiepuff was holding a heavy jacket with belts all over it. Everyone else was in the feast hall, celebrating Christmas Eve at the end of a long toy-building season.

"There it is," said Toffee, pointing to a ripple on the calm sea. The Dauntless emerged from the surface, its autopilot guiding it alongside the dock. Thanks to the automations that Santa had added after that first fateful trip to R'lyeh, the door no longer had a wheel that required cranking to open it. The steam valves released their pressure, and it swung open on its own. Gumdrop's hoarse screams erupted from within as soon as the watertight seal was broken.

"Gently, lads," said Snickerdoodle. Cookiepuff and Toffee descended through the hatch and lifted Gumdrop out moments later, bound up in the straitjacket and twitching like a garden gnome who'd been drinking syrup all day.

"Going to be a rough week," said Toffee. That was usually how long it took before Gumdrop's screaming abated.

Snickerdoodle nodded. "It's a good thing that Cookie Congress isn't in session between Christmas and New Year's. His constituency wouldn't like it if they weren't properly represented."

Finding a pair of jobs for Gumdrop hadn't been the hard part, after all. Cthulhu still needed his coal delivery as long as he was on the Naughty List, and it wasn't as though Gumdrop was getting any madder. One job down and Snickerdoodle thought, "Where would Gumdrop's madness blend in well, and cause the least disruption?" His first campaign had been a roaring success, and no one even thought about challenging Senator Gumdrop when he ran for re-election.

Snickerdoodle became the second elf to retire from the toymaking profession, Gumdrop having been the first. She still practiced law, and her second job was taking care of Gumdrop. She had dinner at Santa's table once a week, as a token of the jolly old fellow's gratitude for the sacrifices she'd made over the whole affair.

And in R'lyeh, Cthulhu continued his aeons-long slumber, blissfully unaware that a mantle had been erected, a stocking hung from it, and the pile of coal within it grew just a bit heavier every year. Well, perhaps not blissfully. *Horrifically* unaware, then.

TIDINGS OF THE NEW MOON
Alcy Leyva

As soon as Glenn heard the keys turn in the lock, he staggered backward as if the cold, steel teeth were entering his heart instead of his apartment door. Outside of the window, light snow drifted silently in the moonlight like souls falling lightly from heaven.

You can do this, Glenn told himself. *You can do this. You can do this.*

The truth was that Glenn could not do this. In fact, his track record had already proven that there wasn't much in his life that Glenn could do.

Growing up had been hard on Glenn. The runt of his litter, his seven other sisters and brothers had fumbled over him when he was first born. And that was only the beginning. When he had turned one—a strapping young wolf pup with his entire life ahead of him—his father had shoved him into a lake. While his father would have been quick to say that the "shove" in question was more of nudge just as much as the "lake" in question was more of a puddle that had welled up in their backyard, Glenn remembered it differently. He would say that if he hadn't been struggling in the first place, he wouldn't have fallen out of his father's mouth and into the deep, dark abyss and nearly drowned. It would have saved him the near-death experience. And the therapy costs.

This was Glenn's way of dealing with life—a personal philosophy. Life was something that was constantly happening *to* him, leaving him with very little to say in the exchange. Even in his adult life—even after marrying and raising five wild pups of his own—Glenn had resigned himself to this fate and not asked any more of the universe.

The situation he had found himself in, as well as the secret he was keeping as his well-established family came spilling through the front door, was a prime example of this resignation. And, like most matters, it made everything worse.

Ellaine walked in, eyes dark, her mind seemingly set on the next conquest on her To-Do-List. She said nothing and worked diligently, passing the yapping pups through the door, then dropping her purse and laptop off into the corner before setting the family's dinner by the side table. She swatted the front door shut with her tail, all in one massive maelstrom of motherhood.

Glenn just watched, his eyes half-lidded, as Ellaine tumbled through these acrobatics with the faint acknowledgment that her husband was standing there in the shadows.

The pups barked and bounced around the apartment. They chased each other around Glenn's legs and nibbled on his tail and ears. Glenn watched each one with prickling anxiety. One huff from their mother extinguished all of this frantic energy and sent the little ones dashing upstairs to clean themselves before dinner.

"You all right?" Ellaine called over as she heaved dinner onto the large wooden table in the dining room. Glenn realized it was Wednesday—deer night. His wife had brought in a rather large sport for the evening. With nothing but deep teeth marks drawn around its broken neck, the deer's lifeless eyes stared back at him. Glenn observed how its pelt was intact and none of its organs were flopping out. It was a perfect kill, and judging from the crimson lipstick Ellaine was wearing, Glenn figured she had caught it on the way home.

"Glenn?"

"Um. Yes, yes. I'm fine. H-how was your day?"

Ellaine hesitated. Looked at him up and down. Cocked her head.

"Your ear is twitching."

"Excuse me?"

"Your ear, Glenn. It's twitching. The same way it twitches when you have something to say and don't want to say it."

"Don't know what you're talking about," Glenn replied, setting his paws on his head to pin his right ear down. It was, in fact, trembling like a scared rabbit.

But Ellaine wasn't having it. She stalked around the table toward him. Nervous, Glenn stammered. "I-I must not be feeling well."

"You're sick?"

"I'm..." Glenn couldn't find the words. "I haven't been feeling well since—"

"What is that?" Even from the distance, Ellaine had spotted the slight discoloration of the fur around Glenn's neck. What was typically charcoal black and shiny (Ellaine insisted Glenn use a special shampoo to keep his dander in check) had a blue hue running from his nape to his throat. The skin beneath was cracked and puss-filled.

"Glenn?"

"Honey, I have something to tell you." As he turned around, Glenn spotted the moonlight reaching out to him through the nearby window. The snow had already reached nearly five feet, but through the clouds, only the round moon commanded the sky. There was a silver sheen on its full face which seemed to bathe everything it touched with an ethereal glow.

Glenn backed slightly away from this moonlight as if it

were fire threatening to consume his flesh and, gathering his strength, he straightened his back and stood proudly as he said, "Tonight I went out to the woods to get a Christmas tree."

Ellaine glanced over at the tree slumped in the corner of their living room. It was a beautiful tree with pristinely bristled leaves, surrounded by a thick odor of pine which filled up the entire home. Wads of melting snow still clung to its branches.

Before she could open her mouth, Glenn pounced on her words. "I know, I know. You sent me to the store to pick one up. But as I was walking down there, I remembered what you complain about around this time: every year you say that you want a real tree. And, every year, something happens and it never fits the budget. So, I decided to go out and get one ... for free."

Ellaine cocked her head to the side again. "You actually went out and got a real tree? From the woods, Glenn? It's snowing like crazy tonight."

Glenn looked from side to side. "I thought it would be easy. So I drove out to the woods up north. Took my bow saw. Walked in three feet of snow. I spotted a tree I liked almost instantly. And it was actually pretty simple to saw it down. But before I get it back to the car...."

Glenn could feel his wife leaning in. She was almost looming over him.

"... before I could get it back, I was ... attacked."

"Attacked?" Ellaine's voice prickled somewhere between shock and suspicion.

"I didn't see it right away," Glenn continued. "It snuck up on me. I was busy dragging the tree down the hill, keeping my balance. But before I knew it, the damn thing was right on top of me, Ellaine. Right here. Snarling. Scratching. I couldn't defend myself."

"What was, Glenn?" Ellaine begged. "What was on top of you?"

He stared deeply into his wife's yellow eyes and replied, "A human."

Ellaine's jaw dropped as she mouthed the words. "A human."

Glenn's voice dropped to a whisper. "A female, wild as can be. She was naked, blonde. She pinned me down and sunk her teeth right into my neck."

Glenn reached up and pawed at the wound. Watching his wife, he suddenly felt as if time had frozen. Ellaine did not blink. She did not move an inch. She took forever to respond. And when she finally did, it wasn't with a question he was expecting. "And then what?"

He fumbled with his words. "What?"

His wife was now a few paces from him, edging ever closer. "She bit you but … then what happened?"

"She-sh-sh … she bit me and then ran off into the woods."

Elaine blinked slowly. "So, the story you're telling me, just so that I can fully digest the weight of your words here, is that you went out to the woods…"

"Yes."

"… were attacked by a human…"

"Good so far."

"… were bitten by said human …"

"Sure."

"… and then the human ran off and disappeared?"

"Exactly!" Glenn shouted, feeling the relief of this admission flowing through him.

Half-eyed, Ellaine looked back at the tree and sucked her

teeth. "Is that why our hardwood floors are now covered in melting snow?"

Glenn stammered and stuttered as Ellaine turned her head and howled for the kids to come down for dinner. Then she looked back at her husband and sighed to herself. "I don't even know why I get suckered into your stories all the time."

"This isn't a story, Elaine. I was really attacked by a human out there."

"Please, Glenn. Trying to cut corners because you're too cheap to pick up a real tree and getting bit by a naked floosie is hardly a bad day. *I'll* tell *you* about a bad day."

She never got to tell this story as the small storm of pups scurried down the stairs and took their places on one side of the table. Ellaine spread the deer's belly out and the young ones dove right in. Just a few light claws and nibbles tore open the thin flesh, spilling the warm, succulent guts out onto the table with a wet splosh.

One of the pups, snout dyed a deep crimson, turned back to his father and licked the grime from his teeth. "Coming to eat, Dad?"

Feeling his wife's eyes on him, Glenn dragged his paws to the table and sat. All of his pups were too into the dinner to notice that while he was indeed present, their father was not eating. Actually, the sight of the mutilated animal was turning Glenn's stomach. Maybe it was his two daughters playing tug-of-war with a thick section of intestines. Or the steady patter of blood and bile tapping onto the floor. Maybe it was the smell—the coppery stench of raw meat—hanging the air. Whatever it was forced him to turn his head.

"What's gotten into you?" Ellaine asked. Glenn realized she wasn't eating either. All of her time now seemed taken up by staring intently at her husband. Glenn could immediately relate to the dead deer on the table.

"Actually, I think I'm going to lie down," Glenn declared, pulling away from the fresh game. His kids paid him no mind as he slumped by, tail dragging wistfully on the ground behind him, though he could feel the eyes of a cold huntress on his back as he slowly climbed the stairs.

THREE NIGHTS LATER, ON CHRISTMAS NIGHT, WHEN THE MOON AP-peared like a white cat curled about a black shadow, and while his entire family was tucked away and deep in their own quiet pockets of sleep, Glenn dreamed an impossible dream.

In this bizarre world—a world he at first thought was a fabrication of his own imagination—Glenn found himself running through a green glade of grassy hills and plains that rolled for as far as his eyes could see. He could hear the breath flushing from his mouth. He could feel his legs pumping against the soil. He could even feel the sun's rays reaching down on him from above.

But this was all a lie.

Pulling back, Glenn realized the green glade was actually a projection on a 60-inch flat screen television. This TV was set into a square cut-out in a wall at the front of the room. In this room, facing this scene, were thirty treadmills with human men and women running on them. Some had headphones wedged into their ears. Most had large sweat stains blooming out of their pits. Everyone was running.

Glenn looked down and realized that he, too, was running on his own treadmill and was suddenly filled with dread. Not because the motorized whir of the tumbling leather strip beneath his feet seemed unending. Not because his heart seemed to be crawling out of his throat with each and every step.

No, it was the nature of Glenn's body that filled him with fear. The body running beneath him was not his own. Gone was his furred torso and claws. Gone were his whiskers and fangs.

Glenn's legs were hairless. The two naked stalks of flesh ran down and ended, not in padded paws, but in flat feet stuffed into sweat-soaked socks and cross-fit sneakers. His chest was broad and wrapped in a drooping shirt. His arms, measly and fleshy, pumped against the air in time with his knobby knees and ankles. The way his head bobbed back and forth, seemingly connected to his torso by a thick hose of meat, made Glenn nauseous.

And he suddenly saw more.

He saw himself creeping along on silent bookstore visits. He saw himself standing in line at the DMV, and licking postage stamps, and coughing up bad sushi trips, and late night taco runs.

Glenn woke up screaming, his fur matted in sweat. El-laine just tossed over and gave him her back.

In the darkness, Glenn's mind was racing. To him, this dream was proof that the attack he had suffered over a week ago—and the bite he had received in the woods that night—had been the catalyst for a disturbing change in him.

In stories growing up, Glenn had heard of people turning into supernatural creatures.

But what was this?

In these dreams, Glenn had turned into something far more absurd and therefore something far more frightening.

Whatever had entered his blood that night in the woods was threatening to turn him into the supermundane.

Glenn sat patiently in the waiting room, listening to the receptionist tap dutifully away at her desktop computer. His ear, which hadn't stopped shaking since he woke up that morning, danced to the beat of her clicking claws on the keyboard.

Twenty-seven and a half minutes later, Glenn was sitting across from his boss as the oversized hound read over his paperwork. Phil was the CEO of Glenn's pack. He was also twice the size of Glenn and so muscular that his brown fur sat on his bones like rolling mounds. Watching this hulking wolf carefully paw through his documents reminded Glenn of the day Phil became CEO—the day he tore out the throat of Glenn's previous boss. It was during the staff holiday party. Glenn's Secret Santa got him socks.

As a backdrop, the wall behind Phil's desk was adorned with the stuffed heads of every trophy kill his boss ever got. Deer, raccoon, skunk ... hell, even turtles and squirrels. Glenn counted fifty-two different species in total. It was obvious that Phil had immense pride in the things he killed and made sure to flaunt his alpha-ness however he could.

Not even looking up at him, Phil asked, "Glenn. How was your Christmas?"

"Actually, rough. My wife left me a few days ago and—"

"Good, good," Phil said without hearing, flicking through the papers. "Why is this is a letter of resignation?"

"That's because it is, sir. My resignation, I mean." Glenn tried his best to keep eye contact, except it only made his eyeballs itchy.

"Mhm." His boss looked down at the papers. "Resigning due to 'medical reasons.' What does this mean, Glenn? Are you sick?"

"I—"

But his boss quickly cut him off with one claw. Summoning his secretary, Phil walked out from behind the desk and paused to look out of the majestic thirty-foot-tall windows overlooking the city. He truly was massive for a wolf, almost ten feet tall. He rested a paw on the pane and his amber eyes twinkled, framing him as if posing for a surprise photo shoot.

Outside, the city of skyscrapers (and the tiny dots of wolves creeping along the sidewalk) seemed to give off a glow that brought out the highlights of his boss' fur.

"Do you know how I got to be CEO of this pack, Glenn?"

Glenn nodded only to catch a glimpse of where his ex-boss' head hung quietly between a bison and a cross-eyed deer.

"Hard work, Glenn, plain and simple. This time last year, I was one of the rank-and-file like you. But now look at me."

The secretary walked in and carefully placed a round glass basin underneath where her boss stood. Without missing a beat, Phil began urinating in it while telling Glenn, "And you know what I never had?"

Glenn strained to hear the question over the sound of the stream filling the glass and just answered, "What is that, sir?"

"Sickness, disease, or maladies—I've never had any time for it," Phil replied. "I've never been sick. I've never had a cold, a toothache, a sprain. My body is completely immune to infiltrations of my bloodstream."

"I get the point, sir."

"And do you know why?"

"No, sir."

Phil looked back and nodded as the level of the urine slowly crept to the top of the bowl.

"Two words you need to familiarize yourself with, Glenn: sheer and will. I demand myself to be healthy and so I'm healthy. I don't have time to waste on sickness. Some stupid bastards say, 'So what? I'm sick for only a day.' But guess what? Those hours add up. And while those sickly dogs were losing years on their life, I was working. I was creating. I was *trending*. Mark my words. Only the weak waste their time on sickness, Glenn. True story: a few years ago, I was about to sneeze but I caught it in my mouth and swallowed it. That's called 'efficiency.'"

"Sure," Glenn said, unsure of what to make of this information.

At the exact top of the glass bowl, Phil cut off his stream of urine as if were as easy as flicking a light switch. Strutting away from the window, he stood importantly behind his desk. It was such an intentional and exact urinary cutoff that even Glenn was impressed. His secretary then tipped the yellow liquid into a spray bottle and began spritzing the corners of the office with the acrid mist.

When she was done, Phil instructed her to, "Make sure to get the break room and the cubicles," to which she nodded and exited. Turning back to him, his boss asked, "What do you think I'm trying to say here, Glenn?"

"I understand that you don't like the idea of me resigning, sir, but I am sick. Last week, just before Christmas, I was a bit—"

"What the hell?" Phil leaned forward. "Is that a bite on your neck?"

"Y-yes, sir. That's what I was about to say. I—"

"Why is it gray and swollen like that? What did that to you?"

"I-I-I was about to tell you," Glenn stammered. "I was attacked by a human woman in the woods. She bit me on the neck and I've been feeling terrible ever since. I've been having weird dreams and sensations. My whole body burns at night. And the moon…the moon feels like it's crushing me. Like the moonlight is rotting my blood. I feel like my body is rebelling against who I am. Like my bones and teeth and hair are sticking in my soul like pins. Ever since this bite, I feel as if I'm losing myself."

When he stopped talking, Phil stared at him.

An entire minute passed without a word between them before Phil took another look at Glenn's paperwork and fetched a pen. On the line for "Reason for Contract Termination" Glenn made out the scribbled response, "Health (mental!)."

Glenn took the signed copy of his resignation letter and walked slowly toward the exit as the mounted heads displayed behind the desk basked in their stuffed glories.

THE RIDE UP TO THE OLD HOUSE WHERE HE'D GROWN UP WAS A long one for Glenn. It took two trains and a rental car to break the vast reach of the city. The drive up made him feel as if he had climbed into one of the old, brown-stained pictures from his childhood. With only a few days until New Year's night—where most of the wolf cities would light up with drunkards and howling to ring in the new year—Glenn felt like he had fallen backward through his timeline. Even the weather had forgotten it was supposed to be winter, with luscious grass lawns sprawling out in front of the houses Glenn passed and balmy 50-degree weather taking up the forecast.

Sitting in the dining room, at his mom's table, watching his mother fix the glasses on her snout the way she always did, instilled in Glenn a dull sense of familiarity.

And this all made him absurdly depressed.

The kitchen was just the way he had left it when he

moved out all those years ago. The drapes were the same. The smell of the table cloths was definitely the same. Glenn had returned to the exact place and time and nature of where he learned about life.

As his mother prepared two glasses of herbal tea, the kitchen speakers by the stove blared out the news. When he was just a pup, these speakers were connected to a little radio with a big fat digital clock on its face. Last year, Glenn had hooked up the entire house to WiFi, eliminating the need for that old radio altogether.

On the news, a burly voiced newscaster was talking about the New Moon coming up. "This will be the first time such a phenomenon has synched up with a New Year in centuries. The New Moon is tied to many myths and legends dating back to the start of civilization. So on New Year's night, just as the ball drops, or as the champagne toast go up in your own private festivities this year, take a look up and—"

"Selene, lower volume to one," Glenn's mother commanded and the reporter's voice dropped off.

Glenn's mother glanced at him over her glasses. She'd always had white fur and soft features, so she always looked young. The only details that gave away her age were the faint wrinkles that sprouted up on the edges of her eyes every time she smiled.

"You're so skinny. What was that wife of yours feeding you, Glenn?"

"Ellaine cooked a lot, Mom."

"I remember your father, God bless him. He once got so sickly and gangly that he could hardly howl at the moon without getting winded."

"I remember," Glenn replied with a faint tapping of his claw on the table. He wanted to avoid bringing up his dad in any way, shape, and form, so Glenn did what Glenn did best: he quickly changed the subject to something worse.

"I quit my job yesterday."

"What!?!" Glenn's mother shook her head. "But why? That job was amazing. You were amazing there. You were *happy* there."

"I just..." Glenn felt as if his words had grown into a dark, foreboding woods in his mouth and there was no way he could find his way out of it. "I needed something different."

His mother waited a heartbeat before slamming her paw on the table and declaring, "Good. You're better than that dead-end pit you called a job."

Glenn was not surprised by this. Ever since he was a pup, his mother was always protective of him. She protected him from any danger and took his side in every fight, even the ones that were logically his fault in the first place.

"I haven't been feeling well." Glenn doubled-back. "I mean, I haven't been feeling comfortable. Just needed a new change of pace. That's why I'd like to stay here a couple of days... If I can?"

His mother nodded and reached over the table, setting her paw atop his. "Live your life, Glenndaline. You only get one life."

Glenn nodded and realized that he hadn't heard his full name used in so long. Leave it to his mom to use the shape of its putrid sound to lovingly club him to death.

"I told this to your father. Told him night and day for years," she added with a hefty bark. "He didn't listen and, God bless him, he's no longer with us. That's why I pray for him every night. Every night."

"I understand, Mom."

"Just do what makes you happy and... Glennadline, your ear is twitching."

Glenn reached up. "Oh. Oh right. It's nothing."

"It means you're not getting enough vitamins in your diet."

"Okay, Mom."

"This is serious. 'Take care of your body 'cause it's the only one you got'. Your father used to say that all the time, bless his soul. Don't be like him Glenndaline. Your father...."

Glenn watched as the whiskers on her face quivered just before she broke down in tears. Glenn cleared his throat and awkwardly flipped his paws onto hers, pressing them together.

"Mom."

Through her sobs, eyes soaked, she looked up. "Yes, dear?"

"I didn't want to bring this up."

"It's fine, dear. You can talk to me. I'm here for you."

Glenn cleared his throat again. "Why do you keep talking about Dad as if he's dead? I can see Dad right there in the backyard."

Glenn pointed out of the window leading out to the perfectly mowed grass. And right in the middle of this sea of green was his father, lounging on a lawn chair as the stainless steel grill behind him smoked with the smell of charred rabbit. With one paw, he chugged a beer. With the other, he waved at the two of them.

"Hey, guys! Burgers are done in ten."

Glenn's mom dropped the shades. "I want to remember him the way he was."

Glenn raised the shades. "But why? He's right there."

Glenn's father waved his empty beer can. "Hey, honey. Would you be a dear?"

The shades slammed shut again. "We all have to mourn somehow, Glenndaline," his mother shouted and jerked her paw away. She then grumbled something about Glenn finishing his tea while dumping hers right into the sink.

As she stormed off, Glenn sighed and pulled up the shades once more. He had actually come back home to talk to his mom about what he had decided to do with his life; the entire trip—just for her. Little good that did.

Leaving the tea behind, Glenn stood up from the table and opened the fridge. With a can in hand, he walked out onto the lawn where his father greeted him with another light wave.

"Guess your mother had something better to do," he said taking the beer and opening it.

"Guess she did," Glenn responded.

"What got you up here so early, Glenn? Was expecting you and the kids here after New Years."

"I—" Glenn began and then faltered. Looking at his father, still a large, proud brown wolf, a lump swelled in his throat. This image clashing with the black leather straps and thick chains of the collar bound around his neck made Glenn feel as if he was the one who was choking to death.

It had already been a few years since Glenn's dad had been diagnosed, though if you asked Glenn, the old wolf had started losing his signature curly smile and the sharpness in his eyes long before that. Old wolves tended to lose a lot of their wolf-dom when they got up in age, slowly slipping back into the days when their kind was more wild and uncivilized. While this was no secret, and while Glenn himself had always been aware of this happening to people around him, he never thought it could happen to *his* father.

Spotting his son's reservations, the old wolf cracked a smile. "Don't worry about me. What's on your mind?"

But just before Glenn opened his mouth, he watched as

his father's eyes grew distant, glazed, as if a slow eclipse had shaded his mind. His tongue flapped out of his mouth. His tail began to wag. He looked like he wanted his son to pet him.

Then he snapped back into his own mind, his own place, as he added, "You can tell me anything, Glenn."

"I—" Glenn began again and was ready to stop, but then it all spilled out. The Christmas tree. The woods. The naked human woman. The attack and the bite. He talked about Ellaine taking the pups and leaving. He talked about quitting his job. All of it spewed out of his mouth like a fiery volcano of self-doubt and misery.

His father took the last sip from his beer and got up from his lawn chair. Glenn took note of the chain scraping against the ground as he passed. Patting his son on his head, the old wolf cracked open the grill and squealed with delight. Wafting away the thick pillar of smoke that was curling up into the air, Glenn spotted a few family staples slowly cooking on that grill. Alongside the steaks and burgers, grilled rabbit ears were wrapped in charred aluminum foil.

"Look at this spread, huh? You know I once saw you eat all of these in one sitting. Ten. I couldn't get them off the grill fast enough." He grabbed a pair of steel tongs and began flipping them. "Almost done. Al-most."

"Dad?"

"Yup."

"You're not going to react to anything I just told you?"

"Probably not." Then, seeing the concern on his son's face, he bellowed out a laugh. "Aw c'mon. Lighten up. Was just pulling your tail." Throwing his arm around Glenn's neck, he said, "Look, I get it. Things aren't shaping up for you in the present. Look at me! I'm not exactly in the best of spaces either. But things are going to work out, for both of us. You'll see."

At this, Glenn's dad reached up with his leg and began scratching the back of his ear with it.

Glenn glanced over to make sure his mother wasn't watching from the kitchen window.

"I have no idea how you can be so optimistic about this. Especially with this," Glenn said and kicked the chain so that it rattled. The end of it was bound to a metal spike embedded deep into the ground.

"It's not so bad. She set up the grill nearby so I can work my magic on the weekends. And when it rains, she lets me go inside. It really isn't—"

"I really don't need to hear that 'It really isn't that bad'. That's the last thing I need to hear right now."

But Glenn's father wasn't listening. On the other side of the yard, just around the outskirts where the green met the dead trees of the nearby woods, a squirrel had come scampering out.

Going back to the place he went to in his mind, his father dropped to all fours and bound toward it. Just as he was about to tear the little guy apart, the slack on the chain disappeared, stopping the large wolf in midair and driving him into the ground.

Confused, Glenn watched his father get back to his feet and limp over to the lawn chair where he collapsed in a huff.

"Dad?"

"I'm okay," Glenn's father replied, waving him away before his son could draw closer. "I'm all right. Just tired 's all. You gotta..." He pointed around in no particular direction, "You gotta not give your mother anything to worry about. Just ... it's alright. All of this is all right."

"But I'm not going to be all right," Glenn protested. "I'm not. This bite... Dad, I'm not feeling like myself. I keep having these dreams—"

"Dreams? What dreams?"

"Dreams where I'm not myself. I'm not a wolf. I dream of being ... a man."

Glenn's father shook his head. "What do you do as a man?"

Glenn started pacing. "Antique Roadshows and opening up cafes with weird names for coffee. Like 'For the Luv of the Nut' with it spelled l-u-v. And 'Roasty n Toasty.' And driving a Prius."

Glenn's father huffed. "What's a Pree-oos?"

"I have no fucking idea." Glenn grabbed the side of his head and dug his nails so deep into his skull that he thought he could feel the bone underneath. "I feel like I'm slipping, Dad. Like whatever this is, whatever I'm becoming, is a monster. Just like what attacked me. I'm becoming a monster, Dad. That's why I just need a few days to stay here. Get my head clear. I won't be staying long."

Glenn looked back only to see that his father was no longer listening. Sitting on all-fours, the older wolf was staring intently into the dead woods overlooking the yard. With the collar still firmly on his neck and the chain coiled in the grass, he stood with perfect posture. His ears were perked up to their highest points. In the distance, Glenn caught the chatter of birds in the branches and the rustle of leaves. He wondered if this is what his father was searching for or if the squirrel from before had returned. Either way, the conversation was over.

Glenn reluctantly walked over and placed a paw on his father's head, but the old wolf didn't respond, never broke his sightline to the trees.

IT WAS TRADITIONAL FOR WOLVES TO GATHER THEIR FAMILIES AND friends on New Years. To surround themselves with their loved ones and bring in the new year with much food, flair, and fanfare. The females would bring the games, the males would set the times, and quite often, everything would fall into a beautiful rhythm of chaos and dancing and howling by the night's end.

Instead, three days after sleeping in his old room in his parents' house, Glenn took the morning to walk out of his room, out of the front door, and into the unforgiving trail. He had used the excuse that he needed some air and space to breathe, but the truth is that Glenn had no idea what he really needed. So he just started walking. In no particular direction or with no certain goal—just walking forward instead of backward for a change.

Glenn had walked on the street for a while, but when the paved roads of civilization ended, he found himself on a clear path out to the bigger houses sitting out in the outskirts of town. When these paths ended, Glenn figured he had gone this far and had no reason to turn back so soon.

By the time the sun had set, the loud boisterous voices of other wolves getting a jump on the New Year's festivities were replaced by the calls of the wilderness, and eventually, by nothing.

After twelve hours of walking, Glenn found himself so far outside of town that he couldn't even see the lights from the windows. He could hear the rush of a nearby stream, the smell of a deer that was just there a few minutes before him, and the swaying of the dark branches in the wind. But there was no one else. Just him.

"I should get back now," Glenn said to no one. Then he

realized he had nothing to go back to. Not a family. Not a job. Like a wound he had created, his life had sealed itself behind him, still festering yet now forever closed. He looked up at the night sky but didn't see the moon. Only gray clouds covered the sky for as far as his eyes could see, like a robe to wrap the dead.

And that's when the snow began.

Though he was out in the middle of nowhere, it was definitely a nowhere he had been when he was younger. A favorite hunting spot of his father, Glenn remembered there was an old bridge nearby that ran over the roaring river that cut down the state like a gash. He walked there without knowing what to expect and therefore not expecting to know everything that was to happen next.

About an hour later, Glenn found himself staring over the side of the bridge from his childhood. Though he could see nothing but black emptiness below, the slip and slosh of the river called to him. Cold and hungry, his breath came out in large billowing bursts that ran up the sides of his face. Arms tucked against his chest to keep his heat, he listened to the low hum of water down below. He wondered what time it was. When will the new year begin? Would he see it?

Glenn stepped out to the edge of the banister and balanced himself, the roar of the water coming up to greet him from the darkness like applause.

The snow was only up to an inch but it made Glenn's life miserable. The wet state of his legs and chest seemed to crunch down on his bones. His breath was coming out more labored and desperate, and there was pain rattling up his spine that felt like a hot blade was trying to pry him open.

Then the new moon appeared. Like a black eye, it burst through the dead cloud cover and seemed to peer directly down at a single most insignificant spot on the planet: Glenn.

In the wake of the moon's view, the pain that blasted itself into every inch of Glenn's body sent him tumbling down and over the edge of the bridge. And, instead of falling for ages before crashing head-first into rapids, Glenn—almost instantly—fell into two feet of water and a few jagged rocks.

Fortunately, the last time Glenn was at this particular bridge, he had been only a third of his current size. Which meant that what had appeared to be a vast gorge to a tiny pup was nothing more than a hollowed out hill with stream snaking through it to a full-grown wolf.

Shaken up by the impact, Glenn tried to crawl to his feet but found himself overcome by the will of the moon. Lips foaming, he felt his insides seize and pull everything—his intestines, stomach, liver—right into his chest. This sent a thick stream of vomit from his mouth that splattered on a nearby rock. He felt both of his ankles break, and then his legs, and then his hips as tiny explosions tore bone, cartilage, and muscle alike. Pieces of his flesh and fur peeled off and fell in chunks onto the ground as if he were being scalped by an invisible knife. His ears collapsed from his head. His tail dropped to the floor.

Screaming, Glenn fell in a heap until the attack on his body was over.

After what felt like an eternity, Glenn was finally able to open his eyes. He was still out in this unremarkable woods and it was still snowing. Around him, Glenn found himself surrounded by large bloody heaps of rotting skin and fur—his, he realized. Standing up, he discovered that he had been changed. He was pink and fleshy. A man.

Under the new moon, had become a man.

Suddenly, Glenn heard something out in the darkness. His eyes could no longer see into its reaches, nor could his hearing or smell tell him what was coming. But it was a single figure, stepping toward him on the highest part of the ridge.

It was the human woman. The one who bit him.

She grasped a tree to lean over and look down at the pieces of the wolf he used to be.

Glenn wasn't sure how it was possible. He had first come across her almost a hundred miles from they were now. How did he find him? *Why* had she found him?

The woman looked down at the man he had become and said nothing. She was still naked but didn't seem to care about the cold chill surrounding her. Her blonde hair waved at Glenn as the wind swirled and then, as if this was all she needed, she pulled back from the ridge and disappeared from view.

Glenn tried to call out but his mouth and teeth felt alien. He made a low muffled groan and few grunts, but it didn't make sense to his ears.

Abandoning the husk of his body, Glenn tried his best to scramble back up the hill to catch the woman, but just like his mouth, his legs and arms didn't seem capable of quick movements at all. Glenn fell face first into the dirt, flopped back onto his legs, hit a rock, and toppled backward. Without fur, the snow and wet soil on his skin cut through him like glass.

Glenn gathered himself and set on all fours to climb his way out. Luckily, with the extra traction, it only took him a few minutes to manage the feat. When he was done, the muscles and fibers in his new body burned with exhaustion. He wanted nothing more than to sit down and rest, but there was someone waiting for him there.

The blonde woman was sitting on a rock looking rather

bored. Spotting Glenn, she immediately hopped up on her toes and walked over. Helping Glenn to his feet, the woman then brushed off the mud stains from his knees and chest. As she did, Glenn looked around shocked by how dead and lifeless the woods seemed without the senses he had before. It all seemed flat and quite average. He also attached a sense of fear and dread to this dullness because what else would the unknowing world feel like to someone who was just born?

When the task of cleaning him up was done, the woman nodded and then, without saying a word, she began walking back into the words.

Glenn looked around the dark trees again as she walked away, unsure of what he had to do next. Where could he go? What did all of this mean?

Several yards away, the woman stopped. Several other figures soon came out of the shadows around her. Ten, fifteen, twenty. Men and women. All naked and caring nothing about it. They stood around her for a long time, not saying a word. Then after what seemed like ages, they retreated. With her eyes looking wild in the new moon's light, the blonde woman turned to Glenn and extended her hand to ask, "Are you coming?"

Glenn realized that his old life had ended. His family had moved on. His career had been shredded down to thin strips and left to flap in the air. Even his mother and father, for better or worse, had moved on. And, what lay ahead of him wasn't beautiful or grand or even a better life than the one he had had before. It was still strange and dull and complicated. Very little made sense, but then again, he always rode shotgun in his own life—always relied on gravity to keep him lashed to his mundane timeline.

Glenn reached up to grab a twitching ear but found

nothing but empty air. Looking down at his hands, he moved each digit and watched them curl. Then, without knowing why, Glenn turned to the woman responded, "I'll be right there."

MOVIN' ON UP

Laura Morrison

CINDI FLUNG OPEN THE WINDOWS OF HER SECOND-STORY apartment and smiled as a light, balmy breeze from the ocean kissed her skin. The sun was shining from a cloudless sky, the birds were singing, and children were laughing as they played in the neighborhood park across the street.

She leaned against the windowsill and took a moment to soak in the beauty of life. The palm trees along the street were decorated with Christmas lights. She just positively loved that. Having grown up in Michigan, she couldn't get over how cute it looked to see Christmas decorations in a subtropical setting. South Florida was lovely in winter.

Just absolutely, perfectly lovely.

Cindi wished with all her heart that Fate would allow her to stay in South Florida for the rest of her life.

Cindi's wish was about to come true.

She was going to die in twenty-two hours and three minutes.

AH, SCENIC HELL. CIRCLE NO. 4. THE WASTELANDS OF PERPETUAL flame. The fiery meteors crashing to earth. The packs of rabid dogs. The rivers of lava, lakes of boiling oil, and flesh-searing acid rain. The free jazz blaring from speakers on every street corner. Fun fact: while free jazz has only been around in the land of the living for a few decades, it's been on a 24/7 loop in Hell for three eons, give or take a few centuries. This was a plus for the many, *many* free jazz musicians in Hell, but on balance it was still worth it.

Abagail, Ravi, and Cornelia had been among the damned plenty long enough to know the ropes, so when they'd been summed by the President of their hovel association, they'd decided that making the trek to the rental office together would be a good plan. Three fiery scimitars are better than one, as the old saying goes.

Secretly, Abagail was planning on shoving Cornelia to the rabid dogs if it came to it.

Secretly, Ravi was planning to do the same. Cornelia was a weakling.

Secretly, Cornelia had packed some rancid meat and stuck it in Abagail's and Ravi's backpacks when they had been looking the other way in response to her exclamation of, "Gosh, guys—look! It's Vlad the Impaler!" Ravi and Abagail couldn't smell the rancid meat over the sulfurous odor that permeated Hell, but the rabid dogs loved the stuff and would maul the—well, *hell*—out of Abby and Ravi to get at the meat while Cornelia ran for it. She may have been a weakling, but she was crafty and dead tired of her pals throwing her under the bus on their outings.

"Did the President tell either of you what this meeting's about?" Abagail hollered over the wailing saxophone. One would think that the residents of Circle No. 4 would have worked out some sort of sign language to communicate over the free jazz. One would be wrong. A few eons back, it had been attempted, but Satan hadn't appreciated his residents' ingenuity and had had their hands chopped off.

Cornelia and Ravi shook their heads.

"Have you guys committed infractions?" Abagail yelled.

Her companions shrugged, and Ravi hollered back, "Probably!" There were so many infractions in Circle No. 4, it was impossible not to commit one occasionally. But, for the most part, there was only retribution when the President needed to make an example of someone.

They walked on without any further attempts at conversation, which was for the best since their senses were more productively used watching out for rabid dogs and errant fireballs crashing to Earth.

As they walked down the uneven, dusty path between the hovels of their neighbors, they scanned through the smoky haze with watchful eyes, scimitars at the ready.

After a ten-minute walk, they saw the rental office up ahead. It was the only structure in the whole neighborhood that wasn't a mere lean-to pieced together with bones, trash, and mud (made of mixed blood and dust). The rental office was an actual, honest-to-goodness building— small, windowless, and made of gray stone that must have come from a quarry in some other Circle because the earth in Circle No. 4 was all red. Though the building was tiny, it was common knowledge that the basement was labyrinthine and vast.

The ragtag trio scurried through the iron door without knocking, since knocking wasn't really a thing in Circle No. 4. The free jazz made it pointless, and most of the hovels had no doors anyway.

Once the door had clanged into place behind them, muffling the sound of a suffering trombone, Abagail, Ravi, and Cornelia stood around for a few moments waiting for their eyes to adjust to the darkness and lack of red haze. The comparative cool and quiet of the rental office was always a relief to the residents of the neighborhood, even if they knew that they were shortly going to be tortured in the basement for committing an infraction.

The foyer of the rental office was small, with room only for the receptionist's desk. The receptionist, a tall demon with blue skin and long, curling horns, stood and snapped through pointed fangs, "Took you long enough. The President does not like to be kept waiting."

The three mumbled their apologies.

"Well," the receptionist said, gesturing impatiently to a row of hooks by the door, "Hang up your scimitars! Hurry up!"

They did so, then silently followed the receptionist through the iron door behind his desk. They filed into the windowless office of the President, who was sitting behind his desk, fiddling with a Newton's Cradle desk toy. He looked up at them with calculated disdain, letting the swinging marbles clack together rhythmically into the silence.

The three shuffled about awkwardly under his gaze, while the demon receptionist stood at the door smirking faintly at his boss' show of power.

At last, the President spoke. "Thank you, Matthews. You may go."

The blue, horned demon nodded and exited.

Once the door had clanged shut again, the President stared them all down a bit longer, just for the fun of it. "I do not like when my residents are tardy."

The three made a good show of groveling apologies.

The President held up a hand to silence them.

They obliged, instantaneously.

The President gave a curt nod, then said abruptly, "Come." He stood, and they all scampered after him, back out of the office, into the foyer, and through the door to Matthews' left.

This door the three were familiar with already since it was through this door that the residents of the neighborhood always went when they were hauled in for committing an infraction. It led down a spiral staircase and to a low, long hallway. There were a half dozen doors along the hall, most of which at least one of them had been through before.

To the left was the torture chamber where Ravi had spent a week for committing the infraction of pruning the deadly nightshade that had been getting so out of hand it was beginning to creep across his hovel's entrance.

To the right was the filing chamber—another torture chamber of sorts. Abagail had been forced to do data entry every evening for a year for the infraction of neglecting to laugh after Satan had told a joke when he'd come to give a speech at the neighborhood pavilion.

A few doors down on the right was the Chamber of Consequences, a dreadful little room with a rickety folding chair; one sat in the chair and was forced to watch a film that showed the fallout of all the mean decisions one had made that had steered their soul toward Hell. A nightmarish butterfly effect extravaganza, where Cornelia had learned that (among many other dreadful things) she had set in motion a chain of events that led to one of the bloodiest wars in the history of the planet. After her little stint in the Chamber of Consequences, she no longer complained about being in Hell—she was just grateful she hadn't been banished to a worse Circle.

The President led them on to the very end of the hall, where there was a door that neither Abagail, Ravi, nor Cornelia had ever been through. They all exchanged nervous glances and shrugs behind the President's back as he reached out to open it.

It turned out to be a rather nice little theater with squishy red seats, the kind of room that rich folks had set up in their basements to watch movies—though, Abagail had been alive in the mid-1800s, Ravi the early 1900s, and Cornelia way back in the end of the BCs, so none of them knew about the swanky home theaters of the modern wealthy.

Cornelia hovered by the doorway, a bit terrified that this might be a new spin on the Chamber of Consequences but with comfortable seating. The other two strode right in and sat down at a gesture from the President. Cornelia steeled herself for what was to come and sat down by Ravi.

"Shut up and watch this video. Pay attention to every detail," instructed the President. "While you watch, think of how you would convince the main character of this film that she should choose to go to Hell instead of Heaven." Then, he walked out. That was that. No explanation.

The three exchanged confused looks, but then the video started to play and they immediately stared at the screen. The President had said to pay attention to every detail, after all, and they knew better than to disobey a direct order from the President.

The lights in the room switched off and a screen in front of them lit up, blood red. Black and orange words appeared in a bold font made to look like flames. It read:

BEELZEBUB PRODUCTIONS PRESENTS...
CINDI BACCARAT, CONDEMNED TO HELL!
Starring Cindi Baccarat as Cindi Baccarat
Narrated by Balam, Duke of Hell

"Ooh, they got Balam to narrate!" Abagail breathed.
"This must be a big deal," Cornelia whispered.
Ravi, terrified of breaking rules, remained silent.

Abagail and Cornelia dared to look away from the screen long enough to exchange confused looks, then settled in to watch the film.

IT OPENED TO SHOW A NEWBORN INFANT WRAPPED IN A HOSPITAL issue blanket with a striped blue, pink, and white hat on her head.

"This human child," intoned Balam, Duke of Hell in a voice cold as ice, or better yet, cold as dry ice, "is Cindi Baccarat twenty-four years ago by current Earth reckoning." As the camera zoomed out to show baby Cindi in her mother's arms, Balam spoke on in a voice that would have dripped with disdain for the infant Cindi if a voice so frozen could have dripped. "This human female was born to wealthy parents in what is currently known as the United States of America, a land which you may be familiar with as the producer of a disproportionate amount of new Hell residents in recent decades."

Balam left off narrating for a bit as the film showed a montage of Cindi growing to adulthood. The musical backdrop for the montage was—you guessed it!—free jazz.

While a piano player had a seizure across his instrument, accompanied by a trumpet and saxophone presumably playing two different songs backward in different key- and time-signatures, Abagail, Ravi, and Cornelia watched clips of Cindi's first steps, her first birthday, first day of preschool, other first days of other grades, endless sports games and music recitals, Cindi playing with various friends and animals, and—to the selfish residents of Hell like our trio—utterly agonizing amounts of volunteer work: roadside trash cleanup, soup kitchens, saving up money to buy sheep for disadvantaged families in South America, and on and on and on.

One would think a musical montage would be pretty fast, but this one went on for hours that felt like days. Abagail, Ravi, and Cornelia squirmed in their seats, starving and wishing that they'd thought to pack lunches. They stared with mounting loathing and irritation at this dreadful Cindi woman who, for some reason, was (if the title of the film was to be believed) condemned to Hell. Really, the only thing that kept them from going comatose as they stared at Cindi's parade of good deeds and heartwarming moments was the promise of watching her commit some horrible sin that would negate all this goodness.

Finally, the montage stopped.

Without Cindi having committed any horrendous deeds.

The screen went black.

Abagail, Ravi, and Cornelia perked up, hoping it was over.

But then the screen lit up again, with an adult Cindi walking along a city street, pausing to toss some money into a homeless man's empty cup. Balam, Duke of Hell, began to narrate again, "And this is Cindi today. A student on the road to becoming a human rights lawyer. She volunteers at a local animal shelter in what little free time she has between her studies and her part-time job teaching English to refugees. Tomorrow morning, Christmas Day, Cindi is going to die."

The trio watching the film cringed at the mention of the celebration of the birth of Christ.

Adult Cindi had sleek brown hair done up in a bouncy ponytail, a flowy turquoise sundress, and sparkly green sandals.

Cindi walked into a rundown brick two-story building with a sign over the door that read *Metro Adult Education*.

Inside was a small room with light yellow peeling paint and a sticky-looking green-and-blue linoleum floor. What little furniture there was in this waiting room was mismatched and of the plastic-and-aluminum industrial variety.

In one corner was a fake Christmas tree covered with very handmade-looking ornaments.

Behind a window with a hole in the glass sat a receptionist who greeted Cindi with a grin and a wave. "Cindi! I didn't think you were going to make it tonight!" Of course, since the residents of Hell were from all different eras and areas of the planet, they could not understand modern-day English. Thus, Beelzebub Productions had had to get a Hellese speaker to dub over the receptionist's voice in a gravelly growl.

Cindi responded in dubbed Hellese, her mouth not even remotely lining up with the words spoken in a harsh rasp, "Hi Alexis! I was able to rearrange my schedule after all!"

"Super! Thanks so much, doll. I was gonna have to sub, but I didn't have much time to prep," Alexis said and bit her lip, the voice actor dragging out her line in a bored monotone that went on a good five seconds after Alexis' mouth stopped moving and the camera had already pointed back to Cindi.

"Same classroom as usual?" Cindi's voice actor said in a rush, trying to catch things up.

Alexis nodded. "I'm surprised so many people signed up for a class right before Christmas."

"Right? I thought it'd be, like, one or two. But it's up to ten last I checked the website."

"It's all down to you, Cindi. They love you. You're the best. You've got a real knack for teaching. Sure you want to be a lawyer?"

"Super sure," Cindi answered as she rummaged around in her bag.

"Well, you always have a home here. Remember that."

"You're sweet. Thank you. And here—Merry Christmas!" From her bag, Cindi brought out a small gift wrapped in glittery red-and-green paper.

Alexis said, "Aww, doll, you shouldn't have!"

"Oh, don't be silly! How could I not get you a present? You're, like, the best person ever."

"I didn't get you anything though."

"Oh my goodness, Alexis, don't even. Please. I know very well you're sinking every spare dime into Franny's college fund."

"Sweetheart, all the money I save wouldn't help a shred if you hadn't started that crowdfunding thing for Franny when Mark died."

Ravi, Cornelia, and Abagail exchanged sickened looks. Cindi was repulsively good.

"I want to hurl," Ravi muttered.

Cornelia and Abagail nodded in fervent agreement, and they all looked back at the screen.

Cindi shrugged off Alexis' praise. "It's nothing."

Alexis opened her mouth to answer, but Cindi cut her off with a demand. "Open it!"

Alexis opened up the box and took out a fine gold chain with a delicate heart locket. She opened it up and gasped, "Franny and me! Cindi, it's beautiful!" She looked at Cindi. "I want to get you something. I'll feel rotten if I don't get you anything."

Cindi laughed. "Don't be silly. But if you really want to do something for me, just invite me over for dinner sometime. You're the best cook ever, and I'd like to catch up with Franny."

"Perfect," Alexis said with a laugh. "Franny will love it.

She adores you. Wants to grow up to be a human rights lawyer just like you."

Ravi, Abagail, and Cornelia exchanged another round of sickened looks as they came to a silent consensus: Cindy was the worst. They looked back at the screen as Cindi bounced out of the waiting room and down a hall lined with classrooms. To the backdrop of Cindi starting to teach a class of about a dozen students, Balam, Duke of Hell, began to narrate again. "You may have heard of the Movin' on Up Initiative."

Abagail and the other two sat straight up and looked at each other with cautious excitement. Ravi looked like he was about to speak, but Balam started talking again just then, and Ravi snapped his mouth shut. No way was he missing a word. Not after hearing that this was something to do with the Movin' on Up Initiative.

"For those who do not know or need a refresher, The Movin' on Up Initiative is a program we have in place here in Hell to reward model citizens. Those in the statistical analysis department crunch the numbers to find living people who are on the fast track to Heaven, then we gather up a team—like you three lucky candidates!—to visit this living person the day before their death and convince them to choose Hell instead of Heaven.

"What's in it for us, you ask? Well, the engines of Hell quite literally run on trauma, sorrow, confusion, pain, and so on and so forth. It does our power grid a world of good to get a nice, strong influx of the trauma that comes from a stainless soul who joins the ranks of Hell. These good souls just don't have the capacity to process the awfulness, the poor dears," Balam, Duke of Hell, said with a condescending chuckle. "The addition of one pure soul keeps the lights running for a month. So, all that remains is for you to decide. Will you join the Movin' on Up Initiative? Will you bring Cindi Baccarat to Hell?"

The screen went black. No credits, no music, no nothing.

A few seconds of silence ensued.

Then Matthews, the blue demon receptionist, walked in and strode to the front of the room. He halted in front of the screen, smiled, and asked, "Well?"

"Hell yeah!" Cornelia said. "We'd get to go to Circle No. 3? I am so in." She and Matthews turned to look at Ravi and Abagail, who had not immediately answered.

Abagail was biting her lip and looking at the ground. "Um, is there a catch?" she asked. "Like, if we don't convince her, is there some sort of consequence?"

"Yeah," Ravi chipped in. "Seems like it would be rather—um, *not* in the spirit of Hell—er, if you see what I mean, if there were no consequences for failure."

Matthews shot Abagail and Ravi a look. "Of course there are consequences if you fail, morons. You fail, you spend five decades as a gladiator in the Slaughter Dome."

Ravi and Abagail gasped. Cornelia gave a squeak of fear and said, "Um, actually, in light of that, I think I need to think things through—"

Matthews grinned at her and snapped his fingers. A scroll with yellowed edges appeared in his hand. He unfurled it and showed it to her. It was a contract written in minuscule Hellease. "Sorry, but you don't get to say no, Cornelia. Your verbal agreement is legally binding."

"My—my—verbal agreement?" she whispered faintly as she gripped the arms of her seat.

Matthews cleared his throat and scanned the document. "Yes. Right here. Did you not say, moments ago, 'Hell yes.

We'd get to go to Circle No. 3? I am so in.'?" He peered at Cornelia over the top of the scroll.

She mouthed wordlessly, her eyes glued to his.

He nodded. "On the bright side, though, the consequence for refusal to take part in the Movin' on Up Initiative is also five decades in the Slaughter Dome. So." He shrugged.

Abagail gave a choking sound, then whispered, "So either way, we spend five decades as gladiators being ripped apart by hell-beasts while all the residents of Circle No. 4 watch?"

"Yep," Matthews said. "Well, actually, no. Probably yes, but also there's a chance you might convince Cindi to go to Hell, and if you do that then you can Move on Up."

The three sat in stunned silence.

After a suitable pause, Matthews asked, "Well? Ravi? Abagail?"

Ravi muttered, "Um. Fine, I guess."

Abagail shrugged, then nodded.

"I need verbal confirmation, Abs," said Matthews.

She sighed, "Yes..."

Matthews snapped his fingers and two more scrolls appeared. "Super!"

"What's next?" Ravi asked.

"First thing's first," Matthews said. "Take this bag. It'll come in handy." He handed Cornelia a large, leather bag. She gave it a curious look and slung it over her shoulder. Matthews went on, "I'll take you to a conference room down the hall where you'll plan who goes first and what your plan of attack will be. Then, you go visit Cindi!"

THE SUN WAS SETTING WHEN CINDI FINALLY GOT HOME FROM HER day of teaching ESL and volunteering at the animal shelter.

She was so laden down with Christmas presents from students that she had difficulty unlocking her door, but a kind passerby saw her struggle and offered to hold her armload of stuff while she unlocked the front door.

"Thanks!" she said to the old man as he passed her stuff back to her.

"No problem, kid. Merry Christmas."

"You too!" she said, then went up the stairs to her apartment where she had to put all her things down in order to do battle with her deadbolt, which always required a good amount of jiggling and cursing. As she tried to get her key to turn, she suddenly gave a cry of alarm and dropped her keychain.

For a moment there, she thought she'd seen the reflection of her old roommate, Janice, in the brass number plate on her door. She stooped and picked up her keys, then looked at the number plate and was relieved to see just her own reflection looking back at her.

Janice had died five months back in a car crash. Cindi shrugged off the hallucination—if it could even be called that—and chalked it up to being overtired and the fact that Janice had been on her mind a fair bit as the holidays approached. Janice had been a rather awful roommate, and they'd had zero in common, but that didn't mean Cindi wasn't sad Janice was dead.

Once she was finally inside, Cindi set her presents under her Christmas tree, made some cocoa, and sat down on the couch with every intention of reading a book.

But within minutes, she was dozing.

She'd have fallen asleep if it weren't for a strange whispery sound coming from the direction of her kitchenette. The sound jolted her out of her doze and had her on her feet in a half-second. "Hello...?" she called.

The whispering continued.

Cindi tiptoed a few steps toward the kitchenette, wondering whether she was imagining things. She was about to call the cops when she saw a flickering orange light in the darkness of the kitchenette.

Fire.

With a confused jumble of questions jostling in her suddenly panicked mind, (Why were the fire alarms not working? How had this happened? Was the fire making that weird whispering sound? Why wasn't the fire spreading faster? Where was her fire extinguisher?) she sprinted into the burning room.

What she saw stopped her in her tracks.

"Janice?" she whispered.

For there was Janice—transparent and obviously a ghost—standing by a gaping hole in the floor. Flames were licking the edges of the hole.

The lower level of the building was burning.

Self-preservation kicked in and all thoughts of her dead roommate were driven from Cindi's mind as she turned to flee.

Halfway to the front door, Janice materialized in front of Cindi with a pop.

Cindi screamed and stopped short. "Janice! What—"

"Shut up. And stop running. I'll follow you wherever you run. Give it up."

"I'm running from the fire, not from you!" Cindi gasped as she tried to dart around Janice, who kept floating in front of her, blocking her progress.

"The fire?"

"The bottom floor's engulfed in flame! There's a hole—" Cindi flapped her arms back at the kitchenette.

Janice laughed. "The building's not burning, moron. That fire's a portal to Hell."

"Oh..."

A portal to Hell.

Cindi blinked. "A...portal to...Hell?"

"Yep," the ghost answered.

Cindi passed out.

It took a bit for her to revive and for Janice to explain things sufficiently for Cindi to have a vague idea of what was going on. All Janice's explanations basically boiled down to these basics:

1.   Upon her death, Janice had gone to Hell. This was no surprise to Cindi, and frankly no surprise to Janice either.

2.   Cindi was going to die on Christmas morning.

3.   Janice had come to prepare Cindi for the three demons who were shortly going to be visiting her. These demons were going to try to convince her to go to Hell.

This was a lot for Cindi to process.

It took a few hours.

"I really don't think they're going to be able to convince me to go to Hell..." Cindi said. She and Janice were standing in the kitchenette staring down into the fiery pit that led not to the apartment downstairs but to Hell. Faint cries of anguish echoed up to them, and Cindi was fairly sure she could make out a few writhing, fiery bodies.

"Whatever. That's not my concern. I'm just here as a favor to my pal, Ravi. He figured you'd be more receptive to them if you had a friend prep you for their visit."

Cindi frowned at Janice. "And I'm really going to die on Christmas? Tomorrow?"

"That's what they say."

"Well, shoot."

"You said it."

"Um, do you know how?" Cindi asked, daring to scoot the toe of her left slipper toward the edge of the Hell portal.

"Didn't think to ask."

"How could you not think to ask?"

Janice shrugged. "The living think the way they die is a super big deal, but once it's done and you've got eternity staring you in the face it's really not a big deal anymore."

"But, maybe if I knew how, then I could avoid it."

Janice said, "Maybe? But probably not."

They fell into an awkward silence.

Janice broke it after a bit with a bored, "So, ok then. You cool? Three demons from Hell are gonna come and convince you not to go to Heaven when you die."

"Um, no. I'm not cool."

"Well duh. But I mean, nothing else I can say here is gonna cushion the blow anymore. Yeah?"

Cindi shrugged. "I guess not..."

"Right. Then I'm gonna head out. Gotta get back to my body in time to get a good place in line at the soup kitchen. Last time I was late, I was so far back in line my bread was more maggot than sawdust, I tell ya."

Cindi didn't know what to say to that, so she said nothing.

Janice looked at her expectantly, tapping a transparent foot. After a bit, she said, "No one says goodbye anymore on this stupid planet?"

"Oh. Uh, right. Bye, Janice..."

"Laters. See ya in Hell." Laughing at her own joke, Janice faded out.

Cindi began to pace around, trying to get a hold on her

racing thoughts. Should she call her parents and say goodbye? Should she run? Should she check and see how one committed oneself to a mental asylum since she was clearly insane?

She had just decided on trying to figure out the first steps for checking into a mental hospital when a hand grasped the edge of the fiery pit, followed by another.

Cindi backed up a few paces and watched as a slight, frail-looking lady pulled herself up out of the pit. The lady stood at the very edge of the fire and looked Cindi up and down as she brushed soot off her tattered, grimy rags. She adjusted a leather bag hanging over her shoulder.

Cindi spoke into the silence, "You aren't a ghost."

"Huh?" the lady asked, looking around Cindi's kitchenette with interest.

"You're not a ghost. Janice was a ghost. I could see through her. But you're... real..."

"Yeah. So?"

"You're dead... How do you have a body?"

"Janice has a body too, Cindi. She just projected here because she couldn't be bothered to come physically. Of course, residents of Hell have physical bodies, idiot. If we were just spirits, that would severely limit the forms of torture Satan's minions could dole out."

Cindi winced. "You're not off to a good start if you're really here to convince me to go there." She pointed into the fire.

The dead lady swallowed, bit her lip, and backpedaled, "Oh, it's not as bad as all that. Look, let's start over, okay? My name's Cornelia. I'm here to show you some stuff about your past. Hopefully, it'll help you realize that you should go to Hell."

"Okay... But I feel I should tell you that I cannot imagine how this is ever going to work."

Cornelia shrugged. "Come here."

Cindi eyed the fiery pit.

"Oh, no, we're not going in there. I just need to touch you in order to zap you back in time with me."

Cautiously, Cindi took a few steps forward.

Cornelia reached out and grabbed her arm with a filthy hand.

Suddenly, they were somewhere else. There was no flash of light, no swirling vortex, no fade-out-fade-in to help with the transition. Just, one second, they were in Cindi's kitchenette and the next second, they were standing outside somewhere.

Cindi blinked, trying to figure out when and where they were. They appeared to be in a lush, green forest. The heat and humidity were oppressive. Birds were calling all around them.

"Do you know where we are?" asked Cornelia.

Cindi shook her head. "I have never been here in my life."

"Really? Cuz this is supposed to be a place you'll remember..." Cornelia pulled a scrap of paper out of a pocket and glanced at it. "Oh darn. Oops. Hold on." She grabbed Cindi's arm again, and they were suddenly somewhere else.

And this time, Cindi recognized it.

They were at her old elementary school. In the hall, to be precise, surrounded by motivational posters and adorable artwork. There were also Christmas garlands and snowflakes and Santas scattered here and there.

"Recognize this?"

"Yeah," Cindi breathed. "Wow."

She was staring right at her second-grade self, a short kid with bouncy pigtails and a dress with a sequined gold heart on the front.

"I remember that shirt!"

"Big deal. Shut up and listen."

Young Cindi was standing there, talking to another girl who Old Cindi recognized as her ex-friend, Bree. It took only a few seconds of observation to realize that Cornelia had zapped them back in time to the fight that had ended Cindi's and Bree's friendship.

Young Cindi was saying to Bree, "But it's mean! I'm not going to do it!"

"If you don't do it, I won't be your friend anymore!" Bree shot back.

Tears welling up in Young Cindi's eyes, she said, "Fine! I don't want to be friends with you anyway if you want me to do that!" Young Cindi turned on her heel and stomped away.

"Geez, what was that all about?" asked Cornelia.

"You don't know?" Old Cindi asked, watching her retreating younger self.

"Sure, I know. I just want to make sure *you* know what's going on. Otherwise, there's no point to this."

"Fine. In that case, Bree was a very, uh, territorial friend. She got mad when I played with other kids. She was trying to make me be mean to this kid, George, who I'd been playing with for a few months. She wanted me to do a prank on George and I wouldn't do it."

"Why not?"

"It was mean! And George wouldn't have been my friend anymore if I'd done it."

"So you chose George over Bree."

"I chose a nice kid over a mean kid."

"Do you know that you were Bree's only friend?"

Cindi frowned. "Well, yeah, but that was only because she was so mean that no one else wanted to hang out with her."

"And that was why she clung so tight to you. Right? Because she had no one else?"

Cindi glared at Cornelia. "You're saying I should have sacrificed myself so that she'd have someone to hang out with?"

"Well, sorta. Look, the point of this is, this was a turning point in Bree's life—you ditching her the day before Christmas break. After you stopped playing with her, she went off the rails. Wanna see what her life became when you left her?"

Cindi felt her stomach churn. She'd heard rumors of what had become of Bree and didn't particularly want to see it. "I thought you were the ghost of Christmas past. Not present."

"When did I say I was the ghost of Christmas past?" Without further ado, she grabbed Cindi's arm and they were suddenly standing in a dingy, cold apartment. There was a stained couch, a mess of takeout boxes and paper plates strewn across a coffee table, and a table littered with vaguely chemistry-looking glassware that Cindi assumed must be related to an illicit drug operation.

Cindi heard a voice and then the sound of a key in the lock of the front door. She turned and watched as a skeletal woman in sweatpants and a faded t-shirt walked in, cell phone to her ear and a plastic grocery bag in her free hand. "Damn it, Charlie. How's that my fault? If some idiot's gonna overdose on my stuff, that's his fault. Not mine."

As Charlie responded in tones loud enough for Cindi and Cornelia to hear, Bree went to the coffee table, pushed aside some takeout (spilling rice in the process), and tossed the contents of the grocery bag onto the place she'd cleared.

"Is that..." asked Cindi, staring. "Is that a box of bullets?"

"Sure is," Cornelia answered.

"What's she gonna do with—"

"You'll find out if you just shut up and listen."

Cindi decided to shut up and listen.

Bree was saying, "—then it's a good thing we're getting out of it. Are you ready for this evening? I just got the bullets, so it's all good on my end. You got the ski masks?"

Cindi hissed, "Bullets and ski masks?!"

"Shh!" Cornelia hissed back.

"Great. And Stan's got the car gassed up and all that? It'd be just like him to be the getaway driver for a bank robbery and not think to fill up the tank."

Cindi gaped. Bree manufactured drugs that people overdosed on, and she was going to rob a bank?

"See?" Cornelia said. "You set her on this path. What an awful life. You should be in Hell for this."

"I hardly think it's my—"

"This bank robbery is going to go awful, by the way. She's going to end up shooting eleven people. On Christmas Eve."

"What? She—what? No!" Cindi looked from Cornelia to Bree and back again, spluttering wordlessly.

"And those eleven people have you to thank for it, for sending Bree over to the dark side."

"But—"

"Without your saintly influence, poor Bree went about as bad as you can go."

"But that doesn't mean I'm to blame for—"

"A question for you: What if by you going to Hell Bree could get a reduced sentence?"

"That's possible?"

"Read this," Cornelia said, reaching into her leather bag and pulling out a scroll.

To the backdrop of Bree yelling at the person on the other

end of the line, Cindi grabbed the scroll, rolled it open, and read:

Cindi,

Let it be known that if you go to Hell of your own free will, your ex-friend Bree will be sentenced to eternity in Circle No. 3 instead of Circle No. 7, which is the one she's destined for if she keeps on her current track, which she totally will because she's the worst.

Regards,

Satan

Cindi stared at the signature. "Satan?"

"Yep. Satan. *The* Satan. Cool, right?"

Cindi dropped the scroll like it was what it was. It burst into flame at her feet.

"So, how's that for a deal? You'd be doing Bree a real favor if you went to Hell. And you're so darn nice, how could you pass up that deal?"

"Er..."

"What if I told you the other people we're gonna show you tonight will get the same deal?"

"There are other people I've known who you're going to try to convince me are awful today because of me?"

"You've got it. And you can save them from the really bad circles and let them go to better ones instead! It would be so nice!"

"But I don't want to go to Hell. And it's not my fault if they made bad choices."

Cornelia rolled her eyes. "Sure. Okay. Time to go back to your apartment. Ravi's probably waiting for us."

"You're just showing me one person?"

"Yeah. We've got a deadline. This has to be wrapped up before you die." She put a hand on Cindi's arm, and they were back in Cindi's kitchenette. There was no one else there. "Ravi?" called Cornelia. She wandered out of the room, yelling his name, then came back a few seconds later. "He's not here yet."

Cindi shrugged and leaned against the counter, fighting the urge to ask Cornelia if she wanted some tea. She liked to be a good hostess, but she figured it made sense to draw the line at horrible demons who were trying to manipulate you into burning in Hell for all eternity. "Hey, is Hell really for eternity?"

"Hmm?" Cornelia asked over her shoulder. She was rummaging through Cindi's cupboards.

"Are you really stuck forever in Hell?"

"Yeah."

"Huh." She watched Cornelia for a few moments. "What are you doing?"

"Looking for marshmallows."

Cindi sighed. There was probably no point in mentioning to Cornelia that it was rude to rummage around in someone's kitchen without asking.

Cornelia huffed, "A little help would be nice."

"I bet it would." Cindi crossed her arms.

"Ah ha!" Cornelia exclaimed. "Here we go!" She pulled a bag of marshmallows out of the cupboard above the fridge.

An arm reached out of the fiery pit in the middle of the floor.

Cindi gasped.

Cornelia turned. "Ravi! Hey!"

Ravi climbed out of the pit and brushed himself off as he looked around. He gave Cindi a very unimpressed once over and asked Cornelia, "Has she decided to go to Hell?"

"No. She's tricky. but she'll come around."

Ravi sighed and directed his attention back to Cindi.

"Right. Cindi, hi, I'm Ravi. I'm going to show you some stuff that's currently happening to someone whose life you've totally screwed up. You think you're so great and good, but you'll see what a jerk you are and how it's really justice for you to spend forever in Hell."

"Riiight."

Cornelia and Ravi exchanged a look, then Cornelia stuck a marshmallow on the end of a knife and walked to the edge of the fire pit. "Good luck, Ravi."

Ravi muttered something under his breath, then walked up to Cindi and put a hand on her arm.

In a blink, they were standing in the middle of a crowded room. Christmas music was playing, and there were sparkling lights and decorations everywhere. They'd clearly landed in the middle of a Christmas party.

Cindi spun in a slow circle, looking for a familiar face. "Who's the person I'm supposed to have messed up?"

"There," Ravi said and pointed through the crowd. 'Recognize that guy?"

Cindi saw an old guy in a wheelchair. "Yeah... That's Vern."

"Yup. The dude who you got all that money by winning him that lawsuit against that construction company."

Cindi nodded and walked closer to Vern. He had been paralyzed when he'd been walking by a construction site and a falling beam had landed on him. Cindi had taken on his case, proved that a careless worker was to blame, and that if the company had properly trained their employees then Vern would never have been paralyzed.

He'd gotten tons of money. Tons and tons of it.

Ravi said, "You're wondering what he's done that's so bad?"

Cindi nodded slowly. Vern was talking with a group of people. They were laughing and eating little snacks on toothpicks and having a lovely time.

"Vern's a monster," Ravi said.

"He seemed like a really nice guy…" Cindi said, thinking back to the polite, mild-mannered guy he'd been a year ago when they'd been working together on his case. She hated to think he had some creepy vice that all his money had somehow enabled.

"Sure, he was before he had money. But now he's all kinds of awful," Ravi pointed out. "You know how much cash you won this guy, right?"

Cindi nodded.

"Guess how much of it he's spent to make this world a better place. Go on. Guess."

Cindi frowned. "Not much?"

"Try zero. Zero dollars. He's spent loads of it, sure, but not one cent on anything that's not for him. This swanky apartment's his. He spends half the year flying around the world to fancy vacation destinations. He has a handful of fancy cars. Guess how many houses he owns?"

"I don't want to."

"Three! And he has a yacht."

Cindi sighed as she studied Vern's face. He seemed so happy chatting with his friends. So oblivious. "But he's not being mean! Is he even aware he's doing something wrong by not donating his money to worthy causes?"

"He has nooooo clue," Ravi laughed. "But so what? You don't have to know you're being a jerk to be a jerk. He's totally on the fast track to Circle No. 4. That's where I'm from, so I can tell you with authority that if you can save this dude from it you'd be doing a beautiful thing."

"So...you're trying to convince me that I shouldn't have won him that lawsuit?"

Ravi nodded.

She shook her head. "I'm not buying this. If we follow your reasoning to its logical conclusion, no one should ever be monetarily recompensed for being the victim of something, because they might be irresponsible with the money. That doesn't feel—"

"Look, Cindi," Ravi cut in. "We're not talking about everyone in this scenario. We're talking about Vern, and what a jerk he is, and how you made it happen by winning that case. This poor dude, Cindi. He's so nice to his friends. He pays for their vacations, he takes them to nice restaurants, he makes them all so happy! He's living it up, having a grand life, super happy and stuff. No drugs, no hookers, nothing like that. He probably thinks he's a really good person. But if he'd have tossed, like, a fraction of his settlement at the right charity, he could have sent a gazillion disadvantaged kids to school. Or given so much fresh drinking water to a village in Africa, or whatever. He's gonna be so destroyed when he goes to Hell." He reached into the leather bag and handed Cindi a scroll.

"From Satan?" she asked as she hesitantly took it.

Ravi nodded.

Cindi sighed, unrolled it, and read:

Cindi,

You have set Vern on the fast track to Circle No. 4. Come to Hell and he'll go to Circle No. 1. You owe him. He has no clue what a jerk he's being. He's going to be absolutely destroyed when he ends up in Hell.

Regards,

Satan

"Poor Vern," Ravi said, shaking his head. "Poor, poor Vern."

Cindi said, "But, Ravi. It is not my fault what Vern chooses to do with the money. All that matters, as far as I am concerned, is that I did what I could to help him when he was paralyzed!"

"Whatever, Cindi. You are so selfish."

Ravi put a hand on her arm.

As soon as Cindi realized they were back in her kitchenette, she shook Ravi's hand off her arm and yelled at him, "This is not going to work!"

"She's *still* not convinced?" Cornelia spoke from behind Cindi. Cindi whirled around and saw that Cornelia was still there, sitting cross-legged by the flaming pit to Hell with graham crackers, chocolate bars, and a nearly empty bag of marshmallows beside her.

"No. She's awful," Ravi sighed. "She knows she messed up these people's lives, she knows if she goes to Hell they'll get to go to better Circles, but she's still only thinking of herself."

"She saw the letter from Satan?"

Ravi nodded.

Cornelia responded, "It's a wonder a person as selfish as she is going to Heaven at all in the first place."

"Tell me about it. All she does is blame them."

"But it's their fault!" Cindi growled. "They made the choices that made their lives what they are!"

Ravi said, "Sure, sure. Keep telling yourself that." Then he looked at Cornelia and asked, "Isn't Abagail supposed to be here by now?"

"Yeah. Any time now." She passed Ravi a fork with a marshmallow on it.

He sat down by Cornelia and they began a whispered conversation as they toasted marshmallows.

Cindi promptly tiptoed closer to eavesdrop.

Cornelia muttered to Ravi, "—is never going to work. I mean, do you know if anyone who ever succeeded at the Initiative? Like, has anyone you know ever gone up to Circle 3 for bringing a good person to Hell?"

"Uh, there was that one guy...Darrin? From the next neighborhood over?"

"Really? Sure that wasn't just a rumor?"

"I don't know. But so what? What's your point?" Ravi asked.

"I dunno...It's just...This plan seemed kinda impossible even back in Hell, but now that we're here it seems even crazier. I—" Cornelia stopped short when a movement from Cindi caught her eye. "Eavesdropping? See, you're awful. Heaven people don't eavesdrop."

Cindi didn't bother responding to that and instead jumped in with a question of her own. "What's this Initiative thing?"

"None of your beeswax, that's what," Cornelia snapped.

"Yeah," added Ravi.

Cindi persisted, "Oh, come on, what can it hurt to tell me? Maybe if I knew the whole picture of what was going on here I could, uh, I don't know, maybe help?"

Ravi gave a derisive snort.

Cornelia frowned and looked into the fiery pit. Then she met Ravi's eyes and gave a shrug.

"You think?"

"I mean, there's no harm. Right? And we're running out of time."

"Fine..." Ravi sighed.

With that, they filled Cindi in about the Movin' on Up

Initiative and about how they'd be spending fifty years in the Slaughter Dome.

"Wow…" Cindi breathed. "Fifty years? But wouldn't you get killed after like a day?"

"Except we're dead already, see?" Ravi explained. "So, like, we could get mauled by some big bad hell-beast one day and then by the next we'd have regenerated and we could be thrown right back into the Slaughter Dome. Over and over and over."

"And that was your punishment for if you didn't agree to do the Initiative thingy…?"

"Right," Cornelia said. "And also our punishment if we don't convince you to go to Hell."

"Wow." Cindi found herself feeling a bit sorry for them. Not sorry enough to actually admit it to them, and not sorry enough to go to Hell, but still a bit sorry.

Cornelia snapped, "Yeah. So now you see the full picture. You have all the info. You know what a jerk you're being to us by not going to Hell. You know that we're gonna be ripped apart in the Slaughter Dome for fifty years. And all because of you."

Cindi gritted her teeth to keep back a response that would have done the situation no good at all. She took a steadying breath, and said instead, "Be that as it may, I just cannot imagine that this ever works."

"Sure it does," Ravi countered. "It's just you're a lot more selfish than the other people who've been selected in the past. Most folks, when they find out that they can prevent some people from being ripped apart by hellbeasts day after day for fifty years, and when they find out that they'll have the opportunity to lessen the sentence of people whose lives they've destroyed… well, most folks with that info decided it's their duty to go to Hell for the good of the many."

"But, eternity's a long time. Fifty years is nothing compared to infinity," Cindi pointed out. "And, I repeat, I didn't mess up their lives. They messed up their lives. They made their choices. They—"

"Move over, will ya?" snapped a voice from within the fiery pit.

Everyone looked down.

There was Abagail, hanging at the upper limit of a pull-up at the edge of the pit, but with no room to get out since everyone was either standing or sitting by the edge. Cornelia scooted back and Abagail scrambled out of the fire. She looked around at them. "What's up? You all look angry."

Cornelia jerked a thumb in Cindi's direction. "She's being selfish."

"Yeah," Ravi agreed. "She knows she's going to be sending us to the Slaughter Dome, and she knows she's taking away the possibility of ever reaching Circle No. 1 from the people whose lives she messed up. And she still won't go to Hell."

Abagail looked at Cindy with disdain. "You're awful. Oh my gosh. You do know Circle No. 1 is the best Circle, right? Like the one that's just a step away from the lamest Circle of Heaven?"

"There are Circles of Heaven?" Cindi asked.

"Of course. And probably with every jerk move you make tonight you're falling down a level in Heaven. You jerk."

"Yeah, you're the worst ever," Ravi chipped in.

Cornelia said, "I'd love to sit around telling Saint Cindi what a loser she is, but we're running out of time here."

Ravi said, "You got this, Abagail. When she sees who the next person is, she'll totally fold." He grinned at Cindi and handed Abagail the leather bag.

"That's why we saved best for last," Cornelia agreed.

Cindi felt a stab of nerves. "Who's the next person?"

Ravi grinned. "You'll find out!"

Abagail put a hand on Cindi's shoulder, and they were in the waiting room at Metro Adult Education. At first glance, it looked just the same as it had that morning when Cindi had shown up to teach.

But the furniture was even more worn, and the walls and floor were dirty. The room was much more dimly lit than that morning; about half the lights in the fluorescent fixtures overhead were dead.

It took Cindi a few moments to notice the sound of crying. It was coming from the reception area.

Cindi and Abagail walked over to the desk, and there was Alexis, sobbing, holding a cell phone up to her ear. Alexis had aged significantly. Cindi guessed they were about ten years in the future, though it was hard to judge at that moment since Alexis' face was tearstained and contorted with crying.

"Alexis?" Cindi whispered. "Alexis is going to Hell?"

Abagail shook her head and laughed. "Even better than her. Wait for it!"

At that moment, Alexis wailed, "Franny! How could you do this! How could you?"

On the other end, Franny must have been responding.

Cindi gaped. "Franny? Franny's going to Hell? Alexis' daughter?"

Abagail laughed, "Yes! The little girl you've been mentoring since, like, the day she was born! The girl you've been preaching at about how she should go to college and work hard and blah blah blah, and her life will be just great, and all that."

"You are not telling me that because I inspired her to

go to college she's going to do something horrible and go to Hell."

"That, my dear, *is* precisely what I am telling you." She made a fake pouty face at Alexis and said, "Okay, let's go visit Franny. I just wanted you to get a nice visual of her weeping mother first."

Abagail touched Cindi's arm, and they were in a very classy-looking apartment. The kind with white walls, glass coffee tables, white leather furniture, and shiny silver accents.

Lying on her back on the couch, wearing an expensive-looking black robe, was Franny. She was holding a rhinestone-crusted phone to her ear. "Mom. Stop crying." She rolled her eyes. "No one's going to catch me."

Cindi could hear Alexis' crying through the phone, but couldn't decipher the actual words.

"Mom, seriously! Rich, white people do not get convicted of stuff! It's fine!"

More tearful words ensued from Alexis.

"But see, that's the beauty of it, Mom! Sure, I suspect Ryan's doing illegal stuff, but he's never overtly said it to me, or texted it to me, or emailed it to me, or communicated it to me in any way. So, even if he ever got caught, any accusations of child labor and poisoning the groundwater couldn't be tied to me!"

More muffled words of distress from Alexis.

Franny rolled her eyes again. "Mom. Let me worry about my eternal soul. This is what's gonna be paying for your nursing home. Be practical. And, look, if ForwardTech wasn't doing this, some other company would be moving in and doing the exact same thing. The kids would be working for some other company's factory. The groundwater will be polluted by some other business. That's just how it works in their country. It is happening either way!"

As Alexis responded, Abagail said, "What do you say to that?"

Cindi realized that there were tears in her eyes. She blinked and didn't answer.

"The kid you've been mentoring since forever, convincing her that she just had to go to college. How great is it to see that after you started that crowdfunding college thing for her and raised all that money, she totally succeeded? Great college, great job as a great lawyer with a great company, making great, great amounts of money?"

Cindi swallowed. She still couldn't answer.

"And so what if a few kids get exploited and their drinking water is polluted and they all end up with cancer? Like she said, if her company wasn't doing it, someone else would be."

Abagail looked Cindi up and down, gauging her reaction. Then, with a flourish, she pulled another scroll out of her leather bag.

Cindi sighed, took it, and unrolled it.

Cindi,

Dear little Franny is headed to Circle No. 6 upon her death. But get this: if you agree to come to Hell, I will personally send a demon up to visit her tomorrow and scare her back onto the straight path. All she needs is to be convinced that there is an afterlife, and she'll fall into line, easy as pie. She can right her wrongs and go to Heaven. That's a pretty sweet deal. Save Franny. Come to Hell.

You suck,

Satan

Cindi gritted her teeth and turned away from Franny, who was now full on fighting with her mom, yelling about how awful her mom was for thinking that the only reason

Franny was supporting this was because her boyfriend wanted to do it. "That's an awful thing to say to your only daughter, Mom! My moral compass is not broken! It's not a thing, so how can it be broken?"

Abagail laughed, "Franny's gonna be so surprised when she dies and finds out there's an afterlife. It's so fun to watch the look on the faces of atheists on their first day in Hell." Then she put her hand on Cindi's elbow and they were back in Cindi's kitchenette.

Ravi and Cornelia looked up, their faces eager. "Well?" they asked in unison.

Abagail jerked her head toward Cindi. "See those tears, guys? She hasn't been able to say a word since she saw what a monster little Franny grew up to be."

Ravi and Cornelia gazed at Cindi's tearstained face with joy. "Circle No. 3, here we come," Cornelia squealed.

Cindi shook her head.

Their smiles turned to frowns faster than a hell-beast could grab a victim by the jugular.

Cindi started, "But it isn't my—"

"Cindi," Ravi cut in, his voice frantic. "Franny's exploiting children and giving their village cancer. Doing bad stuff to kids guarantees you at least Circle No. 5. That's all the fireballs falling from the sky, acid rain, ungodly heat, 24/7 free jazz, rotten food, packs of rabid dogs, dirty water, and general filth of Circle No. 4, but with swarms of flesh-eating flying ants and incurable dysentery! That's what Franny's getting. *If* she's lucky."

Cindi mouthed wordlessly for a few moments, wanting to cling to her reasoning that it was Franny's choices that put her where she was, not Cindi's, but the words wouldn't come. All she could think about was Franny.

Abagail said, "Remember, you can actually get Franny to Heaven if you just come to Hell with us."

The three stared at Cindi, waiting expectantly for an answer. They grinned at the tears streaming down her face.

Then, abruptly, Cindi stopped crying. Her face became thoughtful as something occurred to her.

"We've got her," Cornelia whispered.

Then, Cindi began to laugh. Rather bleak laughter, sure, but laughter nonetheless.

The three demons blinked.

"What's so funny, jerk?" asked Abagail.

"Yeah," added Ravi.

Cindi shook her head, unable to respond, so overtaken was she by her creepy, bleak laughter. Finally, only when her three companions had been crossing their arms, tapping their feet, and glaring at her for about a minute was she able to control herself. "See, this is all a big joke," Cindi said.

"No, it isn't," Ravi snapped.

"No. It totally is," said Cindi. "This is all just some new punishment that Satan is doing to you. It's all part of your sentence in Hell. My soul doesn't even figure in."

"Uh, yeah it does," Abagail said. "Why else would we be here?"

Cindi shrugged. "I dunno. It does seem a bit elaborate. But it's the only thing that makes any sense!"

"How so?" grumbled Ravi.

"Well, see, you all live in Hell, which is basically a place that's supposed to be super awful. They stick you somewhere awful, threaten you with that Slaughter Dome thing, and basically delight in being mean to you however they can. Right?"

"Right," they chorused.

"And then they just, what, give you a chance to move to a

better circle? For doing something awful like convincing me
to go to Hell?"

"Yeah...?"

"So you get *rewarded* for doing something so awful as
bringing a good soul to Hell, but I get *punished* for doing the
same thing, condemning Bree, Franny, and Vern to Hell?"

The trio exchanged confused looks.

"Plus, I don't think those notes are even from Satan
anyway."

Cornelia snapped, "Of course they're from Satan! They're
signed Satan!"

"Yeah!" Ravi added.

"Look!" Abagail said and reached into the bag. She pulled
out a scroll and handed it to Cindy.

Cindi,

These notes really are from me.

Regards,

Satan

"Whatever," Cindi said, dropping the scroll into the burning pit in the floor. "That proves nothing. It's a magic bag,
isn't it? You need extra help convincing me of something, you
pull out a scroll supposedly from Satan that backs you up."

Abagail scoffed, "Don't be an idiot. There's no such thing
as magic."

"Says a dead person who's been zapping me all around
time and space."

"The notes are real," Ravi growled.

"Nope. They're not. So all those threats and promises in
them aren't real either. They're not really from Satan."

Cornelia pulled out a scroll, rolled it open, and stuck it in
Cindi's face.

Cindi,

These are so real.

Regards,

Satan

Cindi rolled her eyes. "No, they're not."

Cornelia pulled out another scroll.

Cindi,

They are.

Regards,

Satan

Cindi gave her head one firm shake. "Nope. It's a magic bag. Like that Mary Poppins carpet bag, but evil. You can't convince me otherwise, so just stop with the scrolls. Hell is packed with centuries of evil people. At least centuries. There's just no way Satan has enough spare time to devote to you three and to me. He's got to be busy with more important things, like dealing with all those centuries of evil people." She leaned against the kitchen counter and folded her arms. "Hear me out. Because I bet if I'm right it'll benefit you, too."

They all exchanged suspicious glances. "Go on..." Abagail said, eyes narrowed.

"Okay, so if there's a Hell and a Satan, that proves there's a Heaven and a God."

"Sure. Duh," Ravi said.

"Okay. And God is love."

They all cringed. Cornelia said, "Ugh. Shut up with your cheesy platitudes."

"Shut up with your meanness!" Cindi snapped. "As I was saying... Why would God be okay just letting this happen to me? Or to anyone?"

Cornelia shrugged. "I dunno. Probably he made a deal with Satan."

Cindi countered, "I very much doubt that God makes deals with Satan. Does that sound like a thing God would do?"

"You may have a point there," Abagail conceded. "God is a total control freak. He wouldn't want Satan trying to get any sort of equal power over souls."

"Ah ha!" So you admit God has the greater control?"

The other two shot Abagail a glare.

"I never said that!" she snapped.

"You sorta did…" Cindy responded. "Anyway. Whatever. That's not the point. Let me finish. I think God won't be okay with going along with whatever plans Satan allegedly has to mess with my soul. I don't think God would just let me go to Hell because of some stupid initiative Satan put in place for you. And I think—as you just confirmed, Abagail—God has more power than Satan, and Satan couldn't just steal me. I think you guys are all just pawns in some game designed to torture you more. I think it's really evil of you to try to drag me to Hell just to save your own skins from your Slaughter Dome and get to a better Circle. I think," she said, then paused and gave them all a steady look, "I think…if you guys decided not to try to drag me to Hell, and you sacrificed yourselves for me, knowing the awful consequences, I think that's what would actually get you some kind of reward. But, I also think you won't get any reward at all. Because Hell." Cindi said her spiel with considerably more confidence than she felt. In reality, she was far from convinced she was right. And if the three demons were the ones who were right, her death was mere hours away. If that. It was quite a gamble.

Cornelia, Ravi, and Abagail scooted to the far corner of the kitchenette and began a whispered conversation, with many a glance back at Cindi, who, with nothing else to do, began to make tea.

While Cindi was rummaging around in her tea drawer for some much-needed chamomile, Ravi said, "Hey! Loser! So what if you're right? What does that mean for us? Like, in practical terms?"

Cindi looked up at them. They were all staring at her, looking surprisingly eager for her input. Had she convinced them? "Well... Um, it would mean that while you still have time you should take back everything you said about trying to drag me to Hell. Say something about how you know it's super mean to do that to a person who doesn't deserve Hell, and that you hope I go to Heaven."

They all nodded slowly, looking guarded.

"And also, this should go without saying, but I think you'd have to mean it."

Cornelia rolled her eyes.

Abagail bit her lip.

Ravi scoffed.

Cindi persisted, "If I'm right, it's the only way. What if you choosing kindness is the only way to avoid the Slaughter Dome?"

"But we were explicitly told that by not bringing you to Hell we would go to the Slau—"

"Sure, but that's probably a lie."

Cornelia shook her head and looked at Abagail and Ravi, both of whom looked doubtful.

Ravi muttered, "If you step back and look at the actual facts...then, uh, well, one thing that does seem to be consistent is that doing good things is better for souls than doing bad things..."

Cornelia swallowed heavily.

Abagail shuffled her feet.

Cindi said, her voice dripping with a confidence she

absolutely did not feel, "Well, all I can tell you guys is I'm going to just assume God's going to put me wherever he thinks I belong, regardless of whatever game it is that Satan's playing with you all. So, the way I see it, you guys have a big decision to make, and you'd better make it soon. Do you, in your heart of hearts, want to bring me to Hell? Or do you, in your heart of hearts, think that would be mean? Do you want to not be mean?"

Abagail whined, "What about all those people who you could move up to better Circles though? What about them?"

"I thought I already explained that. I think it's a lie. I don't think it'll happen. Too much of this is hanging on me thinking that anyone associated with Hell is behaving honestly."

"Ugh, I hate you so much," Cornelia grumbled.

"Why? I'm just trying to help."

Cornelia glared.

Cindi added, "I bet I'm not even going to die today either. Mark my words. That's just another lie." The teapot that she'd put on the stovetop started to whistle, making everyone jump. "Tea?" Cindi asked.

"If you have peppermint," Ravi said.

"Same," Cornelia said.

"Do you have rooibos?" asked Abagail.

"Yup," Cindi said, then got to work grabbing mugs and the appropriate tea bags. "So? Not that it matters to me, since my mind's made up to just trust in God—"

"Ughhhhh!" they groaned in unison, rolling their eyes.

"—but what have you guys decided? You only have 'til I die to decide, right? Are you going to be kind? Or mean?"

They gave each other uncertain looks and shrugs.

"Well," Cindi said, pouring mugs for everyone and beginning to pass them out, "I sure hope you choose kindness—"

"Whatever, walking kitten poster," Ravi laughed, but the laugh sounded canned and nervous.

"—because I just don't see how it could be a bad move for you." She handed Cornelia her peppermint. "Careful. It's a little too full."

"Thanks," said Cornelia.

Cindi raised her eyebrows. "Way to go! You said thanks! Did that feel nice?"

Cornelia gave a little jerk of surprise and some tea sloshed out of the over-filled mug.

Cindi, oblivious, turned to get Abagail's rooibos.

As she did, she slipped on the spilled tea, fell backward, and cracked her head on the edge of the marble counter.

She fell to the floor, dead.

The three stood there stunned and staring at her body.

"Cindi?" Ravi whispered after a few moments.

Abagail pushed at the body with her toe.

Cornelia whispered in a panicked rush, "What did you guys decide? Did you decide? I don't know if I decided! I—"

The fire in the pit in the middle of the floor began to swirl counterclockwise, picking up speed fast. Within seconds, it was strong enough to send their matted, filthy hair swirling into their faces. A few seconds more and the s'more ingredients were sucked into the pit.

"What's happening?" Ravi whimpered, backing up.

"It's going to suck us back to Hell!"

Cornelia wailed, "But I don't know what I decided!" She grabbed the handle of a counter just in time, as her feet were pulled out from under her.

With a strangled cry, Abagail was pulled into the flames.

Ravi fell and scrambled in vain on the tiles, then followed Abagail into the fire.

The teacups soared in. The cupboard doors flew open and all their contents were sucked into the spiral of flame.

Cornelia was still holding on to the cupboard door, but she knew it was a matter of seconds. The hinges were groaning.

The last thing she noticed before the door broke off and she was sucked into the pit of fire was that, weirdly, Cindi's body was still lying where it had fallen.

Cindi felt like she was floating.

She wasn't sure how long she'd been wherever it was that she was, but it felt like it could have been seconds or decades.

She did an assessment. Wherever she was, it didn't seem to be hot. That was a good sign.

Or at least, she hoped it was a good sign.

Before she could think further, she became aware of a form materializing in front of her. A guy with a beard and a rather dapper suit.

"Hi, Cindi," he said with a smile.

Was that an evil smile? A kind smile?

"Are you Saint Peter?" she asked. "Please, please be Peter and not Satan."

He chuckled. An evil chuckle? A kind chuckle? "Come on and find out!" and he beckoned her to follow him through the mist.

THE POETRY OF SNOW AND STARS

A Sam Geisler Mystery
Cassondra Windwalker

"ARE YOU SURE THIS IS A GOOD IDEA, UNCLE SAM?"
Parker squinted suspiciously toward the impressive Colonial Revival hotel, with its white columns and sweeping entrance planted incongruously in a bowl of Rocky Mountain peaks.

"I think most people try to avoid ghosts," he went on soberly.

"Whereas your Uncle Sam insisted we pay an exorbitant amount extra for the pleasure of sharing their company." Parker's mother Dani tried to blow her bangs out of her eyes, but her hair was trapped beneath a warm fuzzy hat with a turquoise knit ball on top. She slung a backpack in her son's direction. "Come on, kiddo. Help carry our things inside."

"You two are just grumpy because neither of you could stomach the turns on the way here. I tried to convince you to get some crackers at the gas station before we started into the canyon, but oh, no. You had to get Slushies and candy bars." Clearly unaffected by any motion sickness, Sam Geisler grinned unsympathetically at his sister and nephew. Well over six feet tall and as dark as Dani was fair, he was plainly delighted to be spending the week at the famed Stanley Hotel, known as the setting for Stephen King's *The Shining*.

Dani snorted, but her ire was unconvincing. Not least because as a huge Stephen King fan, she'd been ridiculously easy to convince that the perfect place for their first ever family Christmas vacation was the site of the Great Man's inspiration. The owner of a bookstore deli, Dani was a sucker for all things literary. For instance, she'd had no qualms about insisting her eight-year-old son watch *The Shining* with her over popcorn and ice cream—for research purposes—before they came on this trip. Somehow Sam had wound up being the one with the kid in his bed for a week.

Although Sam had a somewhat regular gig now at the church that had once completely shunned him, he was still living over the shop with Dani and Parker. He could've gotten a second job and moved out, but he kind of liked being a full-time uncle. And Dani was usually glad for his company, although she'd never admit it. Technically, they'd grown up together in a two-parent home, but the reality was that it had been Dani and Sam against the world from the beginning. Sliding back into those roles after Sam's brief hiatus as a husband had been easier than it probably should have been, but hey, good emotional health was for other people.

The lobby of the Stanley was a weird combination of intimidating and highly commercialized, its plush luxury offset by the gift store running a brisk business as customers stomped in with snow boots and ski jackets. Dani eyed the bellhop fiercely and clutched her bags closer.

"You know what the problem with saving your money for a spendy vacation is?" she hissed in Sam's direction, about as quietly as Parker's standard whisper.

"What's that?" he asked.

"You wind up entirely out of your own economic strata."

"Nonsense," said Sam airily. "This is just a hotel, like any hotel. They take money for beds. People get naked, sleep here, shower here, like any hotel. Our money is as good as anybody's."

"If you say so. But hang onto your luggage. I don't want to lose any of the precious stuff paying someone for the privilege of following us to our room."

Sam laughed and shook his head. "You're just anxious because you don't know how much to tip."

"And what if I am? I'm perfectly capable of carrying my own bags. Why would I pay some stranger to do it for me?"

"All right, all right. I promise I won't let anyone else touch our bags. Now, can we check in, or is there someone else you need to glare at first?"

"I'm not glaring! I'm looking unapproachable."

"Oh, you've got that right."

Long accustomed to ignoring their squabbles, Parker wandered the expanse of the lobby with his eyes wide and mouth open, lost in wonder. Sam couldn't blame him. Over-done and pretentious, maybe, but a Christmas wonderland for sure. Trees and lights and ornaments and garlands had transformed the scariest hotel in the United States into the most magical. Sam wondered if the ghosts from *A Christmas Carol* weren't more likely to make an appearance here than any two little girls with blood in their eyes.

"That's the staircase, Uncle Sam!" Parker tugged Sam away from the elevators.

"Why, yes, it is," Sam returned drily. It would hardly have been possible to miss. A huge, sweeping staircase worthy of Audrey Hepburn commanded all eyes, its railings decked with garlands and lights.

Parker pulled a sheet of paper out of his pocket and stabbed at it emphatically. "*The* staircase. Where the ghosts go up and down. We can't take the elevator. We need to take the staircase."

"How about we take the staircase after we get rid of all this luggage? You realize we're staying on the fourth floor, right? I'm sure the ghosts will still be there when our arms aren't full of suitcases."

Four flights of stairs later, Sam and Dani were huffing and puffing, but Parker's excitement hadn't waned in the slightest. This even though he'd walked at least twice as much as his mother and uncle, shooting back and forth across every stair searching for cold spots.

"Here!" he would call out, gesticulating frantically. "The air is definitely colder here."

Dani looked at her brother, eyebrows raised. "How can he possibly feel anything cold? I'm sweating like a horse."

"The power of faith," Sam returned wearily. He reached over and removed his sister's wool cap and tucked it into his pocket. Her fair hair was plastered to her head.

"So you admit that faith is just a placebo that allows you to see whatever you already believe?"

"Clearly you're not tired enough. I admit only that your son is highly susceptible to suggestion."

"Whereas you and the rest of your God-people are all bastions of reason, huh?"

"Hey, I can't vouch for anyone else. And I'm definitely not engaging in a theological argument with you while carrying luggage up thirty thousand flights of stairs in a haunted hotel."

"Fair, fair." Dani subsided and concentrated on breathing the rest of the way to the fourth floor.

Even Dani's grouchiness subsided when they unlocked their room door and stepped inside. Sam had persuaded Dani that there was no point in going at all if they didn't spring for one of the "spirited" rooms where ghosts were said to haunt continually.

"Oh, gosh," she exclaimed, dropping her bags just inside the door. "This is freaking awesome."

Parker followed suit, dashing across the room and leaping onto the huge bed with its carved wooden bedstead with a howl of delight. Sam had to admit the place was impressive. Not overly large, the room nonetheless breathed an impression of lost opulence, of forgotten elegance grown shabby with years. He supposed the Holiday Inn guests would be disappointed in the worn carpet and musty air, but for ghost-hunters, the place was perfect. Sam hauled all the bags over to a corner of the room and piled them up, closing the room door behind him.

Dani sighed happily, throwing back the drapes to take in the stunning view of Estes Lake and the Rocky Mountains blanketed in snow. "Ghosts or not, I love it. Just think, Stephen King was right here when he came up with the story for his book."

"Well, not right here. I think his room was on the second floor. But the fourth floor is supposed to be the most haunted."

"That's right," Parker rejoined, pausing in his bed-bouncing to pull that dog-eared scrap of paper out of his pocket again. "We need to keep our eyes open for a cowboy. And listen for kids' voices."

"That means you'll have to be quiet."

Parker scowled at his uncle, but his face cleared quickly. "Hey, where are you sleeping? There's only one bed."

"Don't you mean, where are *you* sleeping? Why do you assume you get the bed?"

"'Cause it'd be pretty weird if you slept with my mom."

"Dang it. I can't argue with that. But no worries, bud. We have a roll-away bed. You and your mom can have the bed all to yourself. Besides, that mattress looks…historical. I will probably have the better end of the deal."

Dani grinned and went into mom-mode without missing a beat. "All right, everybody. It's already almost dark. Get your stuff unpacked and freshen up so we can go into town and get dinner."

"Don't want to eat in the hotel restaurant?"

"Yeah, Mom!" Parker chimed in. "Let's eat here!"

"No way." Dani's tone brooked no argument. "I'm not paying $50 for a mediocre steak. There are loads of places to eat on Main Street, and I have a whole list of recommendation from online reviewers. Besides, we'll be here for four days. We have plenty of time to explore the hotel."

"Your mom's right," Sam told his nephew. "I was just teasing her. Trust me, you'll like the kids' menus a lot better in town. Besides, I hear they have some terrific candy shops down there, too. And ice cream."

Parker shrugged and ran to his backpack, rummaging till he found the digital camera his mom had gotten him for his last birthday. "Okay, I'm ready."

Dani rolled her eyes. "Fine, food first. I'm starving anyway. And this Penelope's place is supposed to have great burgers."

"And milkshakes?" Parker asked.

"And milkshakes. But if you vote for a milkshake, then that means no fudge."

"Decisions, decisions," Sam said cheerfully. He fished Dani's hat out of his pocket as they headed back out. "I think you're going to need this out there. It's not exactly balmy weather."

Parker insisted on taking the stairs again, but down was much easier than up, especially without armfuls of luggage.

Between holiday shoppers, visitors lining up for tours, and a large party who had just arrived to check in, the lobby teemed with bobbing hats and scarves when they emerged. Sam's gaze stuttered to immobility when it met a pair of worried blue eyes framed by shockingly green hair under a black woolen hat. Something in the woman's expression tugged at him, and he couldn't help smiling reassuringly at her, although he had no idea what she was worried about.

She smiled back, her face clearing somewhat, and Sam was struck by her irregular beauty. Her features were too bold and crooked to be pretty: wide, mobile mouth whose smile was infectious, a nose too large for her face, bright eyes with lids that looked nearly Asian, and a knobby chin. There was a ferocity in her, a quickness, an energy, that drew the eye and made him want to keep watching. That wild hair was the least noticeable thing about her, and Sam almost didn't register her diminutive size of perhaps 5'3". She was obviously a member of the large family group registering for their rooms, and Sam couldn't help wondering if one of the miscellany of adults were her husband or boyfriend.

As he drew level with her in Dani's wake, she grimaced slightly and shrugged in the direction of her group as if to say, "Family, right?" Then he had passed her. Already he felt the loss of their brief connection, and he shivered slightly as they stepped out into the chilly air.

"Dang it!" he exclaimed suddenly.

Dani turned to face him, confusion on her face. "What now? Did you forget something?"

"No, I just realized that anyone who sees us is gonna think we're married."

Parker doubled over giggling. "That's awesome, *Dad*."

"No, it is not awesome."

Dani was laughing too, and she stepped back to put her arm around Sam's waist and lean her head on his arm so she could gaze adoringly up at him. "Oh, come on. What good would it do you to meet anyone here, anyway? We live like a thousand miles away, at least."

"Get off!" Sam yelped, trying vainly to pull his arm away from her octopus-grip. He couldn't help casting a guilty look back at the hotel, but the doors were closed. "I just don't want to look some sort of leering Lothario."

"I didn't realize you were planning on doing a lot of leering on this trip. But hey, you know I'm all for you moving on from the Nurse of Death," she said, referring to Sam's ex-wife Melanie. Melanie was a hospice nurse, and she and Dani had never gotten along. "I'll do my best to look sisterly instead of wifely, whatever that is."

"Great," Sam groused. "Terrific. Don't do me any favors."

Soon they were meandering the crowded, snowy sidewalks of Estes Park, and they all forgot about maintaining any sort of appearances as they dashed from window to window, oohing and aahing over Christmas decorations and taffy-making machines, displays of candy and Native American art, kitschy tourist trap gift shops, and fine silver jewelry stores. Penelope's turned out to be all the reviews had promised, and Parker couldn't resist the milkshakes in the end. He declared he would save the fudge for tomorrow.

When they stomped their way back through the front doors of the Stanley, Sam couldn't help looking around for the green-haired woman, but there was no sign of her or any of her party. Sam swallowed a sigh. Dani was right, after all. What would be the point of meeting someone out here? Of course, there was something to be said for not having a point, for enjoying a flirtation or even just a conversation for the sheer fun of it. He wouldn't have minded trying that out for once.

Since the divorce had been finalized a few months ago, Sam and Melanie had been spending more time together than they had in a long time, and that was not improving his moving-on abilities. Not that they'd been stellar to begin with. He wasn't even sure he wanted to move on, but existing in a half-life as Melanie's friend was enough to drive him to date or drink, and he wasn't sure which would be worse.

Parker insisted they take the stairs up again so he could check for ghosts. Sam quirked his eyebrows silently at Dani but complied with his tyrannical nephew.

"I guess we won't have to feel guilty about how much mountain fudge and ice cream we eat while we're here," Dani offered between breaths.

Much to his gratification, Sam's instincts about the rollaway bed had been dead-on. Its mattress was definitely newer. Parker sat broomstick-straight in bed next to his mother in the darkness, straining his eyes for ghosts, until finally Sam relented and pushed the desk chair with his foot. The slow scrape of wood on worn carpet was enough to drive Parker under the covers and eventually into sleep.

Not an early riser by nature, Sam nonetheless propelled himself up and out of the room before dawn break the next day in hopes of avoiding Dani and Parker's ritual morning drama. He softly closed the room door behind him and headed downstairs, where he bought a cup of coffee and wandered from window to window, watching elk graze outside.

"Good morning," came a soft, slightly Southern voice at his elbow. Almost literally at his elbow, he found, as he turned to find himself face-to-face with the green-haired woman from last night. She really was tiny compared to his rather looming height.

"Good morning," he returned, concentrating mightily on not grinning like a hyena. She was as arresting up close as she had been at a distance, those blue eyes compelling him to tell all his secrets and immediately hide away all at once. For the first time, he noticed a smattering of pink freckles across her nose. "Where's the rest of your crew?"

"Over there." She jerked her chin toward the hotel restaurant. "They all insisted on a huge breakfast before our hike this morning. Well, all except June. She's still in her room. What about you?"

"I left my sister and her son asleep so I could get some coffee in peace," he said, privately thrilled to find a way to slip "she's not my wife!" into casual conversation. "We're supposed to go hiking this morning, too, but I don't think it's anything that requires a carb-load."

"Oh, ours isn't either, but try telling folks from Kentucky that they don't need bacon and biscuits and eggs for breakfast. I'll probably end up having to carry each of them out on my back."

Sam laughed, the image of the diminutive woman before him carrying her family down the trail on her back one at a time too funny to resist. "Maybe you should be the one bulking up."

"No kidding. I'm Delph, by the way."

"Sam. Nice to meet you. Is that all your immediate family in there?"

"Pretty much. My brother and sister and their spouses, and our step-dad. Our mom died about a year ago, and we thought it would be good for all of us to take a trip together."

"I'm sorry to hear that," Sam offered. "It's nice that you're so close. That's not always common with adult siblings."

"You must be pretty close with your sister, too, huh?"

"Yeah, we are. Our parents died when we were young, so we kind of got into the habit of looking out for each other. Plus I'm crazy about my nephew—it's like having this little troublemaker you can simultaneously train and blame for everything."

Delph laughed, turning her head to glance behind her as a taller, slightly chubby woman with a brown ponytail and bright pink sweatshirt came down the stairs. "Oh, there's June. I better start trying to corral everybody, or we won't get on the trails before noon."

"Well, it was nice to meet you. Maybe I'll see you around."

She flashed him a glittering smile, though her eyes remained bleak. "That'd be nice. Maybe we can grab a drink and commiserate with each other later after spending all day with our families."

"That might be in order. I'll keep my eyes open for you."

Sam forced himself to turn slowly back to the window before allowing a goofy smile to crease his cheeks. *That might be in order*, he mocked himself silently. What a dork! But she hadn't seemed to mind.

It was another hour and a half before Dani and Parker were ready to hit the road. The Rocky Mountain National Park began just outside of town, and according to Sam's research, there were a plethora of easy but picturesque hikes at a spot called Bear Lake. So they piled into the rental car with jackets and scarves and mittens and boots and headed down the road. It took longer than he'd expected to get there, and periodically the sun would disappear and a brief snow shower would envelop the vehicle. Parker, of course, demanded that Sam stop the car every time they came to a lookout or saw deer or elk in the meadows or trees on either side of the road, and Sam complied without complaint. What else were they here for, after all? And it wasn't as if they intended to do any serious hiking—more like ambling in the snow.

Sam had read about crowding at the park becoming an increasing issue, so he was pleased to find the Bear Lake parking lot only about a third of the way full. Off-season, he supposed, although RMNP still got quite a few winter visitors.

In typical Mom-fashion, Dani had over-prepared, stuffing everyone's pockets with break-apart hand warmers and attempting to tighten ice cleats over Parker's shoes while he bounced up and down.

"I don't know if we really need cleats in this snow," Sam offered doubtfully. The stuff looked at least six inches deep, and he reckoned it was probably more like a foot deep farther up from the parking lot.

"Better safe than sorry," Dani responded briskly. "When you fall on your ass and Parker doesn't, you'll wish you had cleats too."

"Yes, Mom," Sam returned dutifully, and Parker snorted on a laugh.

By the time they passed the ranger station and reached the trailhead, with its myriad signs promising an abundance of trails in every direction, Dani was already out of breath.

"What the heck!" she exclaimed. "It's not like I'm fat. Why can't I breathe?"

"Maybe you're skinny-fat," Sam offered unhelpfully, easily loping out of reach of her swinging fist.

"No, it's the altitude," Parker said seriously. "We're used to a lot more oxygen in our air, and your body has to work a lot harder because there isn't much oxygen in the air up this high. Most people take a week to acclimate, but we don't have that much time. So we should just drink lots of water. I don't know why, though. Because there's oxygen in water, maybe?"

Parker offered his mother his water bottle, which she accepted with a glare in her brother's direction. "Thank you, Parker. It's good to know there's one gentleman in this family."

"Every family should have just one," Sam agreed cheerfully. "Parker fills the gentleman role, and I have…other duties."

"Huh," snorted Dani. "Well, I vote we start with the Bear Lake loop. It's rated the easiest, and it should be pretty. We can always take another trail if we want when we finish this one, and we can come back every day if we like since the pass is good for seven days."

"Sounds good to me," said Sam. "Then we can head back to town for lunch and maybe some of that fudge."

"Definitely," Parker concurred.

Sam had to admit, even the easiest trail up here did not disappoint. Winding around the verge of the small mountain lake, bounded by pine forests on every side, the path felt like a secret explore in spite of its easy accessibility. The lake itself lay still and frozen, a sparkling expanse of glittering ice and snow. Boulders tumbled around its edge, inviting the bold to clamber up. A brisk wind snapped and snarled at their exposed cheeks, but the sun shone fiercely, sending shafts of color dancing everywhere it touched.

Parker was running several yards ahead, climbing up and down rocks and in and out of snowdrifts, when they reached the junction for the Bierstadt Lake Trail. The wind shifted, striking an eerie note in Sam's ear, and he snatched off his cap, straining to listen.

"Do you hear that?"

Dani paused, head cocked. "I'm not sure. Maybe. Is someone yelling?"

Sam hesitated only a second more. "I think so. Yes. Yeah, I think someone is yelling for help. You stay with Parker."

He took off up the trail, which wound upward almost immediately. Running had been his therapy when Melanie left, but running in snow on a mountain trail was a world away from running down an Indianapolis street. Still, his long legs made much quicker work of the distance than Dani's could have done. The periodic shouts became clearer as he sloshed through, fueling his adrenaline.

"Help! Somebody help! We need help!"

One more bend and he saw them. A huddle of people moving irregularly, jerkily, toward him. His heart sank when he saw a flash of bright green hair under a black cap. He forced his legs to pump harder.

It took him a moment to make sense of the scene when he reached them. Delph, and two men close to her age, were half-carrying, half-dragging a portly older man between them. June, the pony-tailed brunette, her head now bedecked with matching bright pink earmuffs, trailed behind them, her face a swollen red mass of tears. A third woman had been striding out in front, a phone in her hand. She'd been the one yelling for help, and Sam presumed, checking for cell phone reception. When they saw him, the grim little parade ground to a halt, Delph and the two men releasing their burden gently to the ground with groans and sighs.

"What happened?" Sam dashed forward and sank down to his knees beside the unconscious man without regard for the snow seeping into his jeans. Beneath his cap, the man's flabby cheeks were flaccid and gray, the front of his jacket flecked with what looked like vomit.

"Probably a heart attack," answered the slight man nearest to Sam, his blue eyes and auburn hair making him the likely brother Delph had mentioned.

"I tried CPR but nothing worked," Delph added between sawing breaths.

Sam pressed his fingers to the man's neck, searching for a pulse, although his instincts told him the man was not revivable. He already had the look of emptiness. And who knew how much time they had already spent trying to bring him back? Sam made a quick decision.

"Stay here," he told them. "You're only likely to injure yourselves trying to carry him down. You're close to the trailhead now, and it's a short trek from there to the ranger's station. I'll run down and see if I can get a signal, and if not, I'll run to the rangers and get help there."

He didn't state the obvious—there was no point carrying a corpse down the trail.

Delph launched herself at him unexpectedly and wrapped him in a quick, hard hug before stepping back with tears shining in her bright eyes. "Thank you so much."

Sam didn't waste another moment but turned and ran back down the path. Easier than running up, but still no fun in the deep snow.

Dani and Parker were waiting with anxious eyes turned in his direction when he came back into view. He dug in his pocket for his cell phone, holding up his hand to ward off their questions as he hauled in ragged breaths and punched in 9-1-1 with shaking fingers.

Thank God it went through. Sam thought he'd heard that 911 calls were boosted somehow, but he didn't know how that worked. He was just glad that it did. He gave the operator the details and ended the call, promising to remain at the trailhead to lead the first responders to the victim.

Parker's eyes were enormous blue seas of fear when Sam got off the phone.

"There's a dead guy on the trail?" he squeaked.

Sam shrugged. "Maybe. Probably. I think so. Nothing

scary, though, buddy. I think he was probably old and sick, and a hike in the snow was just too much for him. I'm sure he didn't suffer—his heart probably just stopped."

Sam didn't think Parker needed any details, like the frozen vomit that indicated death hadn't exactly been immediate.

"His family tried to help him, but there wasn't anything they could do. I'm going to stay here to help the EMTs know where to go. Why don't you and your mom go on around the lake, and I'll meet you back at the car when I'm done? Here, you can be in charge of the car keys."

Dani's eyes searched his, no doubt looking for confirmation that he was okay. Feigned irritation quickly masked sisterly concern. "Oh, sure, the men are the ones in charge of transportation. That's just fine, but when this one loses the keys in a snowdrift, don't come crying to me because we have to hitchhike back to Estes Park."

"No way!" Parker protested, fear forgotten in the need to prove himself. "I'm not going to lose them."

"I sure hope not. Or the hotel might have one more little blond-haired ghost running around the fourth floor."

Dani pulled Sam aside. "Are you sure you're okay? That's a pretty awful thing to see."

Sam rolled his shoulders and summoned a reassuring smile. "It's not terrific, but right now it feels kind of surreal. And it's not as if I haven't been around my share of dead people. I wasn't expecting it this morning, is all. I'll be fine. You watch the widget, and I'll meet you as soon as I can."

In what almost felt like another lifetime now, Sam had been the pastor of a large community church, and sitting with the dying was not an uncommon task. He'd since successfully sabotaged his entire life, losing his wife and his church in one fell blow. The current position of part-time minister to which he'd clawed his way back didn't carry nearly the same level of responsibility or expectations, but if someone needed comfort, Sam would always be there. Even if he had nothing to say, nothing to do. Job might be one of the most complex books in the Bible, he figured, but its simplest message was unavoidable: in the face of suffering, silent commiseration beat either not showing up at all or showing up with your lips flapping, any day.

"All right." Dani pursed her lips and gave him a quick hug before moving off to follow her son, who was already running down the trail toward the next pile of rocks.

Sam could hear the rumble of a snowmobile as the rangers approached. He waved them down, quickly directing them to where he'd left the stranded family. They roared off in a gust of snow, and Sam reversed direction, heading straight back to the parking lot rather than taking the long way around.

The pristine loveliness of the park had been shattered, the peaceful silence of snow defiled by the engines signaling death on the trail. Sam kept picturing the tableau as he'd first seen it: a woman in a puffy lime coat calling tiredly for help, Delph and what must have been her brother and brother-in-law laboring to haul what had been their step-father to safety, when they had to have known he was beyond help, and June's stricken, grief-swamped face.

What must that have been like, he thought. The initial heart attack, the realization of what was happening, the struggle to save him. Delph said she'd attempted CPR. Had the others tried too? Had they helped her? How long had she pounded on his chest before she'd given up? Who had made the decision to stop? Even though they knew better, they clearly hadn't been able to face leaving him alone out there in the snow, so they'd struggled and sweated, slipped and stumbled, to bring him down the mountain with them. What a terrible, sad story. And to think this was supposed to have been a vacation for a family who'd already lost their matriarch.

It occurred to Sam as he passed the locked-up ranger's station that there had to be some sort of report filed and that they might need his name as a witness. He was pretty sure he'd told that to the 911 operator, but he still pulled a tattered business card out of his pocket and stuck it on the window ledge with a scribbled note: "I'm the guy who called 911 if anyone needs to talk to me." Hopefully, the wind wouldn't blow it away. He wedged it under the window as best he could.

He only had to wait a few minutes for Parker and Dani to emerge from the trail. Parker seemed fully recovered from the shock of learning there was a dead man on the mountain, and Sam felt a rush of relief that he'd insisted Parker and Dani stay behind while he ran on to find the source of the screams for help. Parker was a sensitive little kid, and as far as Sam knew, he'd never been around death. Sam didn't want his first experience to be something like this.

"What do you say we let your mom drive us back to fudge-town, buddy?"

Parker looked skeptical. "You know she drives like a bat in jello, Uncle Sam."

Sam choked on his laughter. "I'm not sure that's the exact phrase, but I'll admit she's got a bit of a lead foot. It doesn't matter in here, though, because we have to drive super slow in the park. Besides, we don't even want to drive fast in here. We could miss something cool." "Don't tell me, tell her!" Parker protested.

"Give me break, brat," Dani said good-naturedly, sliding

into the driver's seat. "I promise to drive so slow, even a snow-shoe hare could keep up."

"Hmmph," Parker grunted, unconvinced. "We'll see."

"How did I wind up with a little old man for a son?" Dani asked Sam rhetorically.

"You'll find that sense of self-preservation very comforting when he's a teenager," Sam assured her.

"Dear Lord," Dani groaned. "Don't remind me. At least I have a while yet to go."

Wood-fired pizza, a box of fudge, and a big bag of caramel corn all but wiped the dramatic events of the morning hike from Parker's mind. Or at least that's what Sam thought. Later that evening, after the conclusion of a highly satisfactory ghost tour that nonetheless produced no actual spirits, Parker asked Sam a question.

"You said those people on the mountain are staying here at the Stanley, right?"

"That's right, champ. But I don't know how long their reservations were for, or if this will mean they have to stay longer or go home sooner."

"I was just wondering, does that mean he'll be haunting the mountain or the hotel? I mean, he actually died out there, but it seems like a lot of the ghosts who haunt the Stanley didn't really die here either."

Sam decided not to be a spoilsport and weigh in with what he thought of the ghost stories they'd just heard.

"I don't think he'll do either, bud. Even in the stories, ghosts stick around for unfinished business. To avenge a wrongful death or something. From what I can see, this guy's time was just up. He doesn't need to haunt anyone."

"Also, ghosts are nonsense," Dani spoke up drily from the other side of the room. "When people die, they return to the earth, Parker. They become the wind and the trees and the flowers. Nothing scary. Something beautiful and alive but in a different way."

"Atheists are no fun in haunted houses," Sam commented mildly.

"Neither are most Christians. Aren't you supposed to leave vengeance for the Lord?"

Sam held up his hands in surrender. "I give, I give. So neither of us believes ghosts are real. But it's much more fun to pretend, especially at the setting of *The Shining*."

"Redrum, redrum!" Parker growled as deeply as he could.

"I'm the one who has to sleep closest to the floor with all the scary shadows," Sam reminded him, mock-seriously. "So keep the nightmarish child-ghost imitations to a minimum, please."

"Redrum, redrum!"

Sam's phone chose that moment to ring, and Parker and Dani collapsed in giggles at his unfeigned start of surprise. He scowled at them and flipped open his phone.

"Hello?"

"Sam Geisler?" a feminine voice drawled hesitantly.

"That's me."

"Hi...um. So. This is weird, but we met this morning? Delph? You helped us on the trail."

"Of course. It's not weird at all." His heart thumped irregularly. "How'd you get my number?"

"You left it at the ranger station, remember? Anyway, I know this sounds crazy, but I'd like to thank you for all your help. Maybe buy you a drink?"

Sam laughed rustily as all the moisture mysteriously disappeared from his mouth. "Ah, sure. That would be great. I mean, you don't need to thank me, but a drink would be nice."

He studiously ignored his sister and nephew, who were making googly eyes and swooning dramatically around the room, respectively.

"Great. So...meet you downstairs in an hour, maybe?"

"Sounds perfect. I'll see you there."

Dani and Parker did their best to ensure that the next hour was one of the longest of Sam's life, which meant that he was more relieved than nervous when he finally escaped their hotel room and went downstairs to meet Delph at the hotel restaurant. She was leaning against the bar, her finger tracing the rim of a glass of ice cubes. Sam was struck again by how small she was and tried not to compare her with Melanie, who was more his physical match with her Amazon height and strong, curvy body. This woman put him in mind of a sexy elf, with her emerald hair and sapphire eyes. A chunky violet sweater that practically swallowed her up and black leggings only added to the impression.

Her lips twisted in a wry smile when she caught sight of him and waved him over.

"I was just about to order another," she said, indicating her empty glass. "What would you like?"

"I'll get it. Gin and tonic?" Sam guessed. "Why don't you find us a table?"

"Sure," she agreed. "Extra lime."

"Gin and tonic with extra lime and a Fat Tire," Sam told the bartender when the man returned. When in Colorado, drink Colorado beer, he figured. Besides, he wasn't much of a drinker. He mostly indulged for the sake of putting others at ease. He did enjoy an occasional beer, but they made him sleepy. Too bad this didn't look like the sort of place to offer a basket of cheese fries or onion rings to soak up some of the alcohol.

"Thanks," Delph said as he brought the drinks over to the table she'd selected, quirking her eyebrows at his glass of amber liquid. "You know that place is supposed to be a high-class whiskey bar, right? I mean, obviously I'm not a whiskey drinker myself, but still…"

Sam laughed. "You'd have me under the table in half an hour if I started in on that stuff," he told her, never one to find his manhood in alcohol consumption. "Not to mention I'd probably cough and sputter all over the table. This will do me just fine, thanks."

She grinned, and Sam was struck again by how a smile transformed her face from merely unusual to enchanting. "Good to know. In case I ever need you under the table."

Sam did choke then, grabbing a napkin and trying to prevent the beer from going all the wrong way down to fill his lungs. "Wow. Didn't see that coming."

Delph sipped her drink. "I could tell. Although to be fair, you probably weren't expecting a full-on flirt just a few hours after my step-father died."

"Hey, everyone deals with death differently. There's no right or wrong way to face grief or even mortality for that matter. How are you holding up? You must be exhausted."

Sam had never been one to waste time talking around tough subjects or pretending everything was okay when it wasn't. In his experience, most people were, pun not intended, dying for someone to speak plainly with. Modern society, for all its pretended openness and shunning of taboos, remained deeply uncomfortable with emotional honesty, with the transparency of basic humanity. So Sam had long made it a practice to always ask the real questions and not ignore the obvious. He'd found that most of the time, given that permission, people almost couldn't resist responding with honesty of their own.

Delph shrugged though, her eyes sliding away from his own. "Tired means I'm alive, right? Could be worse."

"You were the one who performed CPR, right? That couldn't have been easy, especially on a man that size."

"Oh, well…" Her hands fluttered. "I learned in college. I was an EMT for a while. But I never got him back."

An EMT? What was it that drew him to these caregiver types, Sam thought, wondering what she did now. But he wasn't that interested in being drawn into a casual exchanging of details, like jobs and hometowns and favorite animals. He felt a connection to Delph, and he wanted to chase that down, uncover her from the camouflage she wore so boldly that he doubted most people realized that's what it was.

"So death is nothing new for you," he said. Someone else might have found his casualness callous, but he knew first responders were generally relieved not to participate in the double-talk meant to soothe the sensibilities of people who hid continually from their own reality.

"No, it's not," she agreed. "It's never pleasant, of course, but it's familiar. For me, that is. For Zinnie and Ren, Jeff and June…it's different for them. They're kind of traumatized."

"And you're not? I mean, the mechanics may be familiar, but this is still your step-father we're talking about, not some random guy on a gurney."

"Yeah, but…" Her gaze bounced off his again. "I wasn't exactly close to Ike. I know I said he was my step-father, but it's not like I grew up with him or anything. He was only married to my mom for three years. We were all adults. We weren't around much. Not as much as we should have been.

"Anyway," she tossed back her second glass, "you're supposed to be distracting me, not digging around in my wounds with a scalpel. Are you a cop, too, or what?"

Sam laughed. "Nope. Just a preacher of sorts."

"Preacher? Oh geez. No wonder you're a lousy drinker. And what does 'of sorts' mean? Cult leader?"

"Nothing so exciting as that. It means part-time. Have you had to spend a lot of time with the police today?"

Delph tucked her hair behind her ear. "No, not really. Actually, it was easier than I expected. I suppose not a few people have heart attacks in this park. And it's not like Ike was the fittest man in the world. Did they call you yet? I don't know if they'll even need to."

"Not yet," Sam told her, noting that while she'd said she wanted to change the subject, she hadn't. "I'm sure you're right. Sadly. Rocky is such a popular park, and so accessible in a lot of ways, I imagine quite a few folks suffer medical emergencies here. Did you know he had heart problems?"

She shrugged. "Not really. I mean, I knew he was old and overweight, but we picked that trail because we thought it would be an easier one. It was harder than we expected in the snow, though. He seemed fine, until all of a sudden...he wasn't."

Suddenly her expression changed, and Sam twisted in his seat to see what had caught her attention. "Oh, shit," she said, her voice hardening as she got to her feet. "My sister-in-law. I better get her out of here."

June had paused in the entrance to the restaurant. Sam couldn't help feeling sorry for her. Although she possessed none of Delph's delicacy of form, she looked lost and helpless standing there.

"Why don't you invite her to join us?" he suggested, rising himself.

"No way," Delph said. "She's a sloppy drunk. She's not doing so well with all this. I'm going to get her upstairs."

"Sure," Sam agreed easily. "How about breakfast tomorrow? Ditch our respective weirdos and go somewhere in town?"

Delph paused, glancing back at him skeptically. "I don't know. A preacher and a mortician?"

Sam's eyes widened, but he plowed on determinedly. "I promise not to convert you if you promise not to bury me. Otherwise, I can't think of a better pair, honestly."

"All right," she conceded with a faint smile, heading toward her sister-in-law. "I'll meet you down here at seven."

Sam shook his head, sitting back down to finish his beer alone. Dani was going to have a heyday with this. If she thought Melanie was the Nurse of Death, what was she going to say about an actual mortician?

Dani was disappointingly unfazed when he hissed the news into her ear the next morning before slipping out the door. Parker lay fast asleep beside her.

"Ugh," had been her response. "Go away already. I'm supposed to be able to sleep in for once on my vacation. And what did you expect with that green hair? A dental hygienist?"

Delph looked drawn and weary when Sam joined her at the base of the stairs, but he figured it would be impolite to comment on the bags under her eyes. He guessed she'd probably been up most of the night, talking with her family.

"Sorry I'm late," he told her. "Just as I left my room, the police called. You were right—I think they just needed to fill in a couple blanks on their forms but it still took a minute to explain what happened. Rough night for you?"

"I'm the one who was rooming with the dead guy, but June is the one seeing ghosts. That girl—" Delph bit her lip on the thought and shook her head. "It's okay. Being softhearted is not a bad thing. I'm just a little tougher, I guess. And it'd be nice if Ren were better at comforting her than I am."

"Ren? Is that your brother?" Sam held the door open and led the way through the snowy parking lot to his rental car.

"Yeah. Ren, Delphinium, and Zinnia. Mom was an avid gardener and reader of romance novels, so she saddled all of us with impossible flower names. It's awesome."

Sam grinned at her as he slid the car into drive. "I'd say you make it work. You don't make me think of stuffy Victorian ladies."

She grinned back. "No, that's not really my vibe, is it? Ren got the short end of the stick, honestly, especially now that everyone thinks he was named after a Star Trek character."

"Star Wars," Sam corrected her automatically, and she outright laughed.

"Oh, terrific. A preacher and a geek? Things are looking up."

"Hey, geeks happen to have a whole set of skills that the frat boys never needed."

"And look at that. Preachers can flirt, after all. Where are we going for breakfast?"

"How about the Mountain Home Café? It's a little off the beaten path, and I hear they have blueberry pancakes to die for."

"Works for me."

Breakfast was delicious and surprisingly relaxed. Sam had expected this dating thing to be much harder, but Delph's wry, self-deprecating humor and laid-back nature made it impossible not to enjoy himself. He supposed that being surrounded by death all the time forced the things that obsessed most people into a healthier perspective. He tried not to think about that being a characteristic Delph shared with Melanie. The two women couldn't possibly have looked more different: why was he comparing them?

When they returned to the hotel nearly two hours later, Delph's family was waiting for her in the lobby. "Horseback riding," she explained succinctly.

Sam looked at her quizzically, taken aback. She shrugged. "We might as well do something. The body is being flown back home to Kentucky to be cremated as soon as the autopsy's complete. We'll have a service there. And we can't just hang around here thinking about it all day."

"Of course not. Sorry, didn't mean to seem judge-y. I'm glad you guys will still get to spend some time together."

She tugged at his hand. "Come on. Might as well meet them."

As he shook hands and exchanged names and pleasantries, Sam formed swift impressions. He'd been right—the smaller man whose freckles matched Delph's and her sister Zinnie's was Ren. Zinnie's husband Jeff was closer to Sam's size, with hard, cool eyes that matched Zinnie's own. Funny how all three siblings could share the same blue eyes and yet convey such different natures. June still looked lost, a little isolated somehow, even as she clung to her husband's arm, but she smiled and made an effort for Sam's sake.

"You were very kind yesterday," she said. "Thank you so much."

Sam shook his head. "I'm sorry there was nothing I could do. I hope the five of you manage to have a good time out there today in spite of everything. It's incredible how the sun shines here all the time, even with all this snow. You could almost forget how cold it is."

"Almost," she agreed. Her soft voice lacked the southern drawl of the rest of the family, and Sam wondered where she was from, and if that geographical distance somehow contributed to the emotional distance that seemed to exist between her and the others.

"I didn't even ask," Sam said, turning back to Delph. He momentarily forgot to speak as she fitted her slim body to his in a lingering hug, distracted by the slender curves and delicate bones that gripped him with surprising strength.

"Umm...when are you leaving?" he managed, beetle-browing her as she laughed at his obvious derailment.

"Tomorrow morning, alas," she said lightly. "We do need to cut our trip a little short, so we can make arrangements at home. Maybe we can have dinner tonight?"

"Definitely," Sam returned, fighting a blush. Was he really making a date with a woman in front of her entire family? Oh, well. In for a penny, in for a pound. "I'll call you."

Shocked by his own daring, he brushed her lips quickly with his own and strode away before he could make eye contact with anyone, least of all Delph. Unconsciously he raised a hand to his lips. Something powerful, electric, had passed between them in that too-brief moment. And he hadn't thought about Melanie at all.

Well, not till now. Damn it.

When he returned to the hotel room, Dani and Parker were anxiously awaiting his return.

"I'm surprised you're ready," Sam said drily, stepping into the bathroom to brush his teeth. "I thought you needed to sleep in?"

"To be fair, even if I'd gotten up at the cruel hour you first woke me, that would have been sleeping in compared to when I usually get up. And today is our exploring day. We're going to hit every single shop on Main Street. We're going to buy lame t-shirts, candy, keychains, incense, pet rocks—whatever nonsense we can get our hands on. Maybe we'll even find some Rocky Mountain oysters for lunch!"

"What's that?" Parker asked curiously.

"You don't want to know," Sam shouted back through a mouthful of toothpaste. "Even if we find them, no one is eating them!"

"Men," declared Dani smugly, as if that somehow summarized an entire argument.

To his own surprise, Sam enjoyed the shopping day almost as much as Dani and Parker did. By lunchtime, he'd already collected an Akubra hat, a pocketknife inlaid with turquoise, and some chocolate-covered huckleberries, even though he was pretty sure that huckles were a made-up berry celebratized by Mark Twain. He'd even bought a tiny cloth worry doll and slipped it into his pocket, thinking of a pair of troubled blue eyes.

"You're quiet today," Dani remarked, hanging back as Parker lollygagged across over the wooden bridge spanning the creek running through the center of town. "Mooning over your girlfriend?"

"Thank goodness she's not really my girlfriend. I can't imagine what it's going to be like if I ever embark on an actual adult relationship again around you. It's like having a middle-schooler for a roommate."

"Hey, this is me being supportive. You know, like you are with me and Ian."

"That's different. That guy is hilarious. And how can I take anyone seriously whose name is Ian? It's like you're dating Liam Neeson if Liam Neeson were a massive nerd."

"You're one to talk. You might be built like an alpha male since you and Witchface split up and you started hitting the gym, but you are all beta, through and through."

"I have no idea what that means, but I'm gonna assume that beta males are the best."

"Stop trying to get me off-track. Something is eating at you."

Sam shrugged, reluctant to put his misgivings into words. "It's crazy."

"This is you we're talking about. Of course it is. But try me anyhow."

Sam spread his hands and released a slow breath. "Obviously I don't know these people, don't have the first clue about their family dynamic. But something feels off."

Dani shrugged. "I think you've proven more than once that you have damn fine instincts, brother mine. Be more specific. What exactly is off?"

"Everything. Delph tells me they're not really that close, that this guy was only married to her mom for three years. But they all decide to take an expensive family vacation together? And then the one outsider dies, and the only person who seems all that distraught is the one who was probably most removed, his stepson's wife."

Dani's eyes sparked. "Ooh. The murderer-whisperer is back. You think one of them killed the old guy?"

Now that he heard it aloud, Sam wasn't sure if it sounded crazy or true.

"Or maybe..." he said slowly. "Maybe they all did."

"There's the suspicious brother I know and love," Dani said approvingly. "I'll make a cynic of you yet. Now you just need a motive. Oh, and a means. Don't you think the police would have noticed if he'd been murdered? I'm sure there'd have been an autopsy."

"No. I mean, yeah, you're right. There must have been. But we don't know the cause of death. They told me it was a heart attack, but I have no idea. All I saw was the vomit. Which rules out a fall, I guess. There was no head trauma, so they didn't push him. Maybe they poisoned him."

"Poison would still show up in a blood test."

"Maybe. If they were looking for it. I don't know any-thing about poisons. I wonder if morticians have access to chemicals that could kill people."

"Wow, Sam. Quick leap from *have dinner with me* to *did you kill your step-dad*, there. I thought you liked that girl."

Sam pictured Delph, all that fire and fury behind blue eyes, dark-hearted rebel unwilling to relinquish whimsy, a seeming kitten with the claws of a tiger. His lips twisted help-lessly in something between a smile and a grimace. "I do. But to be fair, I don't know her at all. Not really."

"But you find it as easy to think she could have killed as someone as to think she might kiss you."

"To be fair, I think most people could kill someone with enough provocation. And who wouldn't want to kiss these lips?"

Sam pouted, and Dani doubled over with a shriek of laughter that had Parker's head spinning around.

"So, what are you going to do?"

Sam shrugged. "What can I do? I'm not a cop. I don't have access to any of the evidence. I just have a weird feeling, is all. We'll go to dinner tonight, she'll fly out tomorrow, and I'll never see her again."

Dani narrowed her eyes. "If you say so."

Just then Sam caught sight of June, walking aimless-ly along the boardwalk, a steaming paper cup of coffee in her hand. "Hold that thought," he told his sister and jogged across the flagstones to intercept the woman.

"Hey, June," he said. Her eyes shot up toward him, star-tled and, he thought, afraid. "How'd you manage to escape your whole crew?"

She forced a smile. "Family can be a lot sometimes, huh? Besides, they kind of need some time to grieve together. Gave me an excuse to get some fresh air."

"Were you not that fond of Ike yourself, then?"

June's doe-like brown eyes widened even farther. "Oh, no! That's not what I meant. I just didn't know him that well. Ren and I have only been married six months. His mom died a year ago, and I didn't even know her very well. We were... kind of a whirlwind thing, you know?"

She subsided and looked around miserably, as if wishing she hadn't said so much.

"That makes perfect sense," Sam said, even though it didn't make any sense at all. If she hadn't even known the man, why had she been the one so distraught by his death? On the other hand, sometimes it was death itself that was the trauma, rather than the loss of a particular person. "Well, I didn't mean to intrude on your escape. I hope you can enjoy the rest of your afternoon, anyway. I strongly recommend the peanut butter fudge. It's to die for."

She laughed almost tearily. "You're kind of a bundle of contradictions, you know that?"

"I've been told. I am sorry this has been so hard for you, June, why-ever that is. I'll see you around."

Dani had rounded up Parker by the time Sam turned back around. She cocked her head to the side as they reached him. "Wrangle that confession?" she asked smartly.

Sam rolled his eyes. Parker looked back and forth between the two of them. "What? Another murderer? Was that guy on the mountain murdered? There *is* going to be a ghost! I knew it!"

He punched the air triumphantly. Apparently, Sam's chair-dragging specter had not been sufficient to satisfy Parker's morbidity.

"I'm going back to the hotel to get ready for dinner," Sam told his sister. "You guys have fun. I'll see you later."

"Or not." Dani waggled her eyebrows expressively. "And for a giant, you're such a girl. What guy needs that much time to get ready for a date?"

"You will," said Sam firmly. "And this giant girl needs that much time. Mostly away from you."

"Details. I need the details," Sam heard Parker tell his mother eagerly as Sam strode away. He shook his head, grinning to himself. That kid watched way too much ID channel.

This time Sam beat Delph to the lobby. He was standing by the front doors, idly watching visitors and guests, when she appeared at the top of the staircase. He caught his breath, surprised by the hot rush of arousal that swept him at the sight of her.

Her dress should have been too severe to be provocative: a dark blue and black plaid shirtwaist with a prim white collar, wide black patent leather belt, and short skirt. A tiny black sweater and black tights completed the ensemble, her slim legs disappearing into her chunky snow boots. Her short green hair curled wildly around her head. Somehow she was the most beautiful thing Sam thought he'd ever seen. He half-expected her to disappear, like one of the Stanley's ghosts or some wayward pixie. She met his eyes and grinned recklessly, and Sam had to quell the rising energy below his own belt.

She clattered down the stairs so fast he worried she'd fall, slipping her arm through his as if they'd known each other for years. "Where to, Sam?" she asked.

"I figured we can't go wrong with Italian, unless you have a better idea."

"Italian it is, then."

They ate in a little corner booth at Mama Rose's, drinking red wine and licking garlic butter from their fingers and talking over each other about books and movies, daydreams and nightmares, till Delph put her hand on Sam's thigh and looked him right in the eyes. Her palm burned like fire—a fire he craved.

"What are you thinking, Preacher Sam? I see something dark behind those eyes."

Sam's mouth twisted. He wasn't used to having someone else turn his own penchant for directness against him. Into the fray, then. What did he have to lose?

"Just a minute," he murmured, laying his hand against her cheek and drawing her close. Never dropping eye contact, he kissed her slowly, deeply, drinking from her mouth as if his life depended on it. Those wild blue flames dizzied him, warmed him till he imagined he'd never be truly cold ever again.

When he finally drew back, her hand rose to her lips, and still she stared at him, wide-eyed. Deep sadness moved across her features then, as if she knew what he was about to say.

"I think..." he paused, reaching out to hold that hand between his own. "I think you and your family killed your step-father. I think of all of you, June is having the hardest time bearing up under the guilt, which tells me she lacks the hatred the rest of you must have felt. Poison, probably something that wouldn't show up in a tox screen. You're not idiots, after all, and you plainly planned this out far enough in advance to do it right. The only thing I can't guess is why. Something to do with your mother?"

Delph didn't even look surprised. That something cool and hard he'd glimpsed before slipped into her gaze, though, and she drew her hand away from his. She drew her lips in between her teeth, and for a moment he thought she was about to stand up and leave.

Then she shrugged, coming to some sort of decision. "He killed her."

"He killed your mother?"

"Not just her." Delph's voice was clipped, cold, its Southern edges snipped off by rage. "We tried to warn her. He was a con man. A serial killer, maybe? I honestly don't know if he only did it for the money, or if he got off on the killing, too."

She tossed a measuring gaze around the room and went on. "Mom was his third wife. The first two both died in 'accidents,' too. His first wife died in a river-rafting trip. Second wife electrocuted herself in the bathroom. And Mom...supposedly Mom fell while they were on an Appalachian hiking trip celebrating their third anniversary."

Sam saw the waitress coming with a pitcher of water and waved her off.

"They all had hefty life insurance policies on them, naturally. Ren and Zinnie and I tried to convince the cops, but it was pointless. I kind of think they even believed us, but they couldn't prove it. A woman falls to her death from a steep cliff, with no witnesses, seconds after her husband snaps a smiling selfie on his phone? There'd have been no way to distinguish any bruises she got from the fall from the ones she got fighting him to stay on that edge. Assuming she even saw it coming. He might have just waited till her back turned and shoved her."

In spite of her flinty tone, her eyes had filled with tears. She angrily blinked them away, unwilling to acknowledge they were there.

"So how'd you do it?" Sam asked, his voice gentle and low. "Some sort of chemicals from the mortuary?"

Delph let out a startled laugh. "Oh, no! Nothing like that. Something much more...poetic."

Sam shook his head. "Poetic murder?"

"Shakespeare found it poetic enough."

"Fair point. So…"

"I told you Mom named us after flowers. One of the prettiest and strangest flowers in her garden was monkshood. Heard of it?"

"I'm not much of a gardener," Sam returned, his lips twisting. "I'm guessing it's poisonous?"

"Very. Aconite is the official name. A large enough dose will cause cardiac arrest pretty quickly. Not…instantaneously." Her face twisted, eyes dropping only for an instant before flashing back up to meet his fearlessly. "But he didn't suffer any more than he deserved to. And there's only one test that could reveal it, a test they have no reason to perform. Once he's cremated, this all disappears."

"Does it?" Sam asked, unflinchingly.

"You want me to say that I'll be tormented with guilt. That I need to confess because I can't live with this on my conscience. That the rest of my life will be overshadowed by this secret. But that would be a lie, Preacher Sam, and oddly enough, as you can see, I don't want to lie to you."

Sam turned his hand palm up on the table between them, and slowly Delph restored her hand to its refuge.

"Are you going to tell?"

"Tell what?"

Her lips curved in what was far too sad and sweet an expression to be called a smile.

"But I better get you back to the hotel. You have an early morning."

Her lashes did cloak her eyes then, and Sam flagged the waitress back for the check. In silence as complete as it was companionable, they drove to the Stanley. As they crossed the parking lot, Sam couldn't take his eyes off her, watching tiny snowflakes settle into her bright emerald curls and melt on her shoulders. She seemed awash in starlight and crystals, this tiny creature of death and vengeance.

They didn't speak until they reached her room. She unlocked the door and stood there in the frame, head tilted back, one foot tucked behind the other.

"You know—" her voice was scarcely more than a whisper—"he does haunt me. He sits there, on that other bed and watches me till I fall asleep. I'd guess he's angry, but his eyes are black. Just black holes that I can't see into. He's probably waiting for me to join him in Hell. But I don't care. I'm not scared. And I'm not sorry. But..."

She laid her hand on Sam's chest, and he thought his heart might leap out from behind his breastbone to lie in her palm.

"I am sorry that it cost me you. Not that this would likely have been anything, anyway. Time, distance, all that. But I get it. So I won't invite you in here with me and my ghost. One last kiss, though?"

Sam didn't need to be asked twice, even though his throat was swelling up weirdly as if he wanted to cry. He cradled her face in his hands and bent to taste her one more time. Her hands clutched at his shoulders for dear life, and he thought again of those kittenish tiger claws. They kissed until his entire body was awash with flames, his lungs aching. She pulled back too soon.

It would have always been too soon.

He reached into his pocket, withdrew the little worry doll, and pressed it into her palm. She traced its tiny, anxious face and closed her fingers around it.

Her eyes held his till the door snicked shut.

He must have looked wrecked because neither Dani nor

Parker teased him even once when he came back to the room and rolled right into bed. It was sometime around five in the morning when he jerked awake in the darkness, somehow knowing that her presence had left the hotel.

He slipped out from under the sheets and went to the hotel window, standing inside the drapes to stare out at the starlit snowscape of the wild mountain night. He stood there a long time, eyes burning as he looked for the light of blue and green stars.

SLEEP, SWEET KHORS
Dalena Storm

Sleep, sweet Khors, magnificent one
God who rules the Solstice sun
All these days your name we've praised
But now your work is done

IT WAS THE NIGHT BEFORE SOLSTICE EVE AND UNCLE ALEISTER was getting sicker. He'd been sick for a while already, but now he wasn't waking up. When Iris went to visit him in the hospital with her parents, she stood a few feet back from the hospital bed, watching Uncle Aleister's big belly rise and fall under the lightweight covers. His face had nearly vanished into his big bushy beard, which was as black as midnight aside from a white streak down the middle. Iris could just make out the bridge of her uncle's nose and the way his eyelids flickered while his eyes moved around in his sleep. Sometimes he would twitch or give a little grunt, but otherwise, he never did much of anything at all. He didn't sit up and open his arms and say, "There's my little Iris!" He didn't pick her up and ruffle her hair or spin her around.

Iris tugged at her sleeves and shifted back and forth on her feet. After she and her parents had stood there for what felt like a very long time and nothing of mention had happened, Iris asked, "When is Uncle Aleister going to wake up?"

Her mom looked at her dad, and they did that thing where they tried to talk just using their eyes. Then her mom looked back down at Iris. She looked very sad.

"Iris, let's go home now and we can have a little talk."

"Why?" Iris asked.

"Because… it's complicated."

"Why?" Iris wanted to know.

Iris's mom looked away and stared at the window that covered one wall of the room. It wasn't very late in the day yet, but it was already dark out. Little flakes of snow stuck to the glass.

"You know how it's winter right now?" Iris's mom asked, looking at Iris again. Iris nodded. "And you know how, when it's winter, all the plants stop growing? But then, in the spring-time, they come back to life? Well… sometimes the winter can be very hard on people that are sick. It's like they feel like the plants do. They get cold. And tired."

"Is that how Uncle Aleister feels?"

"Yes… I think so."

"And Uncle Aleister will wake back up again when it's spring? Just like the plants?"

"Well…" Iris's mom looked again at Iris's father. Her eyes got even sadder. "Sometimes, honey, people go to sleep and… they don't wake back up."

Iris frowned. She looked at Uncle Aleister on the bed, at his big belly rising and falling. She imagined Uncle Aleister never getting back up, never opening his arms and picking her up again. This made her very sad. It was so horrible that she started to cry.

Iris's mom picked her up and they left the hospital. Iris cried in the back seat the whole way home. When they got to their house, Iris looked at the Solstice tree in the living room and all the presents underneath it, and all of a sudden the whole holiday seemed like a big lie. She ran to her bedroom and threw herself on the bed, refusing to say anything to either of her parents for the rest of the night.

Uncle Aleister *had* to wake back up. He *had* to. Because if he didn't… well… then Iris was never going to get back up again, either.

THE NEXT MORNING WAS THE MORNING OF SOLSTICE EVE, WHEN lots of company was going to come over to celebrate. Iris woke up as soon as the sun came in through her window, and she was about to hop out of bed and run into her parents' room so her mom would wake up and make her breakfast, but right before Iris's feet could touch the ground she remembered what she'd promised herself the day before.

If Uncle Aleister couldn't get up, then neither would she.

Iris pulled the covers back over herself and closed her eyes. She kept them closed for a long time but she couldn't fall back asleep. She opened her eyes and stared at the ceiling. Outside, as cars drove past, their headlights made shadows from the curtains move across the ceiling and walls.

Iris kicked her legs and rolled from one side to the other. She rolled onto her belly and propped her chin up in her hands so she could stare at the dreamcatcher that hung at the head of her bed. Maybe, at night, big spiders came onto the dreamcatcher and ate all of the bad dreams before they could get to Iris. She kicked her feet, staring at the dreamcatcher and imagining the spiders, and then she heard the door to her bedroom opening.

"Oh—you are awake! What are you doing?"

It was her mom.

"Staying in bed," said Iris.

"I see," said her mom. "Is there a reason you're staying in bed?"

"Yes."

"Okay," said her mom. "Why's that?"

"If Uncle Aleister…" Iris started, but then for some reason she couldn't finish her sentence. Her throat hurt too bad and her eyes were all teary. Her mom rushed over and sat on the edge of the bed, wrapping her arms around Iris.

"If Uncle Aleister can't get out of bed, you don't want to either? Is that right?"

Iris shook her head. "It's not fair!" she managed to say through her tears. "Why can't he wake up?"

Iris's mom continued to stroke Iris's head for a minute without saying anything. Then, after Iris had wiped her eyes and nose, her mom went and got a book off of the shelf. It was the one about the Slavic Gods. Her mom sat back down on the edge of the bed and opened up the book, flipping through the pages until she got to the start of one of the chapters. Then she held the book open so Iris could see. There was a picture of an old man with a big bushy white beard. He looked a little bit like Uncle Aleister, except he was older and not as fat. He was sitting in a chariot and he looked like he was glowing because all around him it was bright yellow but at the edges of the picture it was dark and Iris could see stars.

"That's Horse," said Iris.

"Khors," her mother corrected her, making a sound like she was clearing her throat. "The God of the Old Sun."

"He's the one we have the altar to downstairs. Right?"

"Right."

"What animal is this?" Iris asked, pointing at the winged creature that was pulling *Khors*'s chariot.

"That's Simargl, the lion-dog. Do you want me to read you the story?"

Iris nodded.

Iris's mother waited until Iris got herself comfortable, and then she held the book open and started to read.

THERE ARE TWO GODS WHO RULE THE SUN: THE GOD KHORS AND the God Yarilo. Yarilo is the God of the Young Sun because although the days are short when he first begins to rule, they grow longer and longer until they reach their peak, at which point Khors takes over. Khors is known as the God of the Old Sun because when his reign begins, the days are long, but they grow shorter and shorter after that as Khors loses strength.

The Winter Solstice—the longest night of the year—is the time that the reign passes from Khors to Yarilo. These two Gods are not separate from one another, however, but are in fact aspects of each other; together they represent the young and the old, the light and the dark, the energy of growth and the energy of death. The Winter Solstice is a time of transition and of magic. It is when Khors dies and is reborn again.

Khors has been the God of the Old Sun for thousands of years, and though few people on this continent worship him or even know his name, they continue to benefit from his light every year as winter approaches. Khors drives his chariot through the sky hitched to the back of Simargl, the winged lion-dog. As Khors flies in his chariot all around the world, his flaming body and chariot illuminate each of the continents in turn. Every year when the Winter Solstice arrives, however, he needs to find a place in which to land and then, having landed, to die.

Each year, Khors lands in a new spot. His eyesight is so excellent that if he stands on Mars and looks towards Earth he can see the twitching noses of rabbits in the underbrush. As he grows older, his eyesight grows worse, and so he is never able to be exactly sure where he is going to land. Wherever he does land, though, something significant is bound to happen. It has been said that various miracles have taken place in the cities and towns where Khors has landed in years past. Sometimes he brings bountiful harvests, or mild winters, or simply a long stretch of sunny days. Whatever it is that happens is bound to be a blessing.

When Khors feels too tired to stay awake any longer, he tells Simargl to take him down to the earth's surface. After they land, Khors finds a resting place, and lays himself down and closes his eyes. Thus begins the longest night of the year.

There are many strange things that can happen during the longest night of the year. It is possible to send time spinning in a new direction, or even—some say—to stop it completely.

None of these things is advisable, however, which is why it is important to celebrate the Solstice with family and friends, at home, and to make offerings to the Sun to show your appreciation for all of Khors's hard work. To venture out into the cold outdoors is to invite magic, but also disaster. When the Sun Gods are asleep, the world is unstable.

In all of the years of history, the Winter Solstice has come and gone without anything going terribly wrong. On Solstice morning, Khors rises again with the dawn, but as the young God, Yarilo. As darkness tips toward the light, the energy of the spring grows ever stronger until, at the summer solstice, the balance tips again, and Yarilo once more becomes the old man of winter, Khors.

This cycle has repeated itself every year since time began, and it will continue to repeat itself forever.

"So, Khors dies and then he comes back as someone else?" asked Iris.

"Yes, but that someone else is also him, it's just a younger version of him."

This almost made sense to Iris, but she was having trouble seeing how it worked. More importantly, she was having trouble seeing what it meant for Uncle Aleister.

"If Uncle Aleister dies, will he come back again, too? But as a young man named something else?"

"Well," said her mom, "that depends on what you believe. Some people think that's how it works. But other people think it works differently."

"What do you think?" asked Iris.

"I think it's time for breakfast. Are you hungry?"

Iris's stomach was growling. She nodded. Her mom reached out a hand and Iris took it, and they went downstairs to eat eggs and toast.

They spent the rest of the day getting ready for the Solstice celebration. Four grown-ups were coming, along with two kids. It should have been five grown-ups except of course Uncle Aleister wouldn't be there.

Iris's dad vacuumed the house, and her mom made a ton of stuff in the kitchen. Iris went outside and made a small snowman to stand next to the porch that people would see when they arrived. She gave it a baby carrot for a nose, and two small raisins for eyes, and a bunch more raisins for a mouth. It had a very big smile. Iris smiled back at it, but then she remembered Uncle Aleister and her smile faded.

When the sun set that night, Iris helped her mom light candles around the house. They lit candles everywhere except for on Khors's altar. For the past seven nights they had lit fewer and fewer candles in front of Khors, and now there were none left. When the guests arrived, it would be time to put Khors in his grave, which was a wooden box lined with red velvet.

There was a knock at the door and Iris's dad said, "That's them!" He turned on some music of instruments playing a sad, slow song.

Libby and Emily came in. They were wearing all black, just like Iris and her parents.

"Hi, Iris!" said Libby, when she saw Iris standing at the end of the hallway. "You look nice. I like that dress."

"Thanks," said Iris.

The rest of the guests arrived, including the kids, Morris and Ben, and then it was time to have Khors's funeral. Everyone gathered together in front of Khors's altar, which was set up on top of the big black bureau in the living area. Iris's dad brought over a bottle of alcohol and put a tiny little glass down in front of the wooden statue of Khors. He poured a little bit of liquid from the bottle into the glass, and then he poured some more for all the adults in the room.

The grown-ups held their glasses up in the air and Iris's dad said, "To Khors. We celebrate your life. Now, you deserve to rest."

"To Khors," they all said. The adults drank their little glasses of alcohol while Iris and Morris and James got sips of sparkling cider. Khors was the only one who didn't get to drink, because he was just a statue and he couldn't drink out of a cup.

After they put their empty glasses down, it was time to sing Khors's lullaby. Iris's mom passed out the songbooks. Iris didn't need a songbook—not just because she couldn't read, but because she'd already practiced the song with her mom for the whole last month, ever since it became December.

Her dad turned on the music and they all sang.

When it was finished, Iris's mother picked up the wooden statue and gently laid him down to rest inside the wooden box. Khors didn't have a blanket to cover him or anything, and so he looked sort of lonely and cold.

"Goodnight, Khors," Iris whispered right before her mother closed the box with a snap.

The grave, with Khors now inside of it, was returned to the top of the bureau. Everyone except for Iris walked away to the dining area in order to taste the cheese and crackers that had been put out on the table as a snack.

Iris remained standing, alone. The story of Khors's death and rebirth was still running through her head. In the morning, the old Khors would be gone, and a new, young god would take his place on the altar. But her mom had said it would still be the same Khors. But at the same time, he'd be different. Iris didn't understand.

"Iris?" her mother called.

Iris looked toward her mother, who wanted her to come and set out some plates. They were the nice plates with the blue rims that Iris thought were pretty.

The grown-ups sat at the big table and the kids sat at the coffee table, where they had a good view of the tree and the presents. Morris tried to feed his brother, James, who was still crawling, but James wasn't very interested in the food and instead tried to crawl over and grab the closest present, which had a big bow on top.

"No!" Iris told him. "We don't do presents until later."

James started to cry and so his dad had to come and pick him up and take him away. After that, it was just Morris and Iris at the table. The grown-ups were taking forever to finish their food.

"Hey," said Morris, "do you want to see my globe?"

"Okay," said Iris. Morris went to the doorway where his parents had left a big bag, and a moment later he returned with a large ball that looked like the world. He turned it around so Iris could see one of the continents.

"See?" he said. "That's where we live. This is what America looks like from outer space."

"Cool," said Iris.

They sat down on the floor and pushed the ball back and forth until the grown-ups were done eating. Iris watched it spinning as it rolled across the floor, imagining that she was in outer-space looking down on the world. If she could fly anywhere in the world, where would she go? Iris's thoughts were interrupted by her mom calling out that it was time for apple pie and they should come into the kitchen if they wanted some. Morris jumped up to go get a piece, leaving Iris alone with the globe. Her dad saw her sitting there and said, "Iris, don't you want any?" But Iris shook her head. Apple pie was Uncle Aleister's favorite.

When Iris's mom put her to bed later that night, Iris was so tired she couldn't keep her eyes open. With her eyes still closed, she whispered to her mom, "I wish Uncle Aleister would wake back up."

Her mother's hand lingered on her forehead, smoothing her hair, until Iris drifted off to sleep.

FROM A DISTANCE, KHORS APPEARED TO BE VERY SMALL, BUT AS you got closer you realized he was as tall as a mountain. His beard was as long as a river, and his fingers were longer than even the very tallest of trees. His body was withered like a dried out old reed, but the light that emitted from his body was still pure gold.

"Simargl," called out Khors, his voice a deep rumble of thunder. "Take me down to that forest. That's where I'll rest."

He indicated a spot on the world far below. The Great Darkness was almost upon him.

Simargl folded its furry wings behind it as it dove downward toward the appointed spot, pulling Khors's chariot as fast as a fireball streaking through the atmosphere. Khors laughed as they fell, and the sound was like the ocean crashing on the shore. As they approached the earth's surface, both of them shrank smaller and smaller until by the time they landed Khors was no larger than a man and Simargl was no larger than a mountain lion. The light that emitted from Khors's body was no longer blinding but was like the light that fills the sky just before the stars begin to appear overhead.

Khors could not remember having ever come to this spot before. In almost five billion years, he had still not exhausted all of the different locations on Earth. Yet, just as it had been every time before this one, he had felt called to this location by some kind of meaningful connection. He did not know what that connection was, and perhaps he never would, yet he knew that this was the spot in which he was meant to die.

Simgarl pulled the chariot by foot now, taking them along a dirt path through the woods. Khors looked around with his still-sharp eyesight, and then he saw something that filled his heart with joy.

Lying against a tree-trunk just off the path was a small, square glass bottle labeled "Bourbon Whiskey." The bottle was still half-full of amber liquid.

"Lucky day!" Khors cried out with his rumbling voice. "Someone's left me an offering. It seems that some people must still care for the old Gods after all."

He leapt out of the chariot in a surprisingly fluid motion for such a decrepit old being, and danced over to the bottle, picking it up into the air and examining its contents gleefully before unscrewing the top and taking a big gulp.

Once Khors had finished what was left in the bottle he gave a big, contented sigh. "This is one thing," he said, "that has actually improved over the years. Whiskey. And now, having drunk it, it's time for me to rest."

Khors sat down next to the tree and fell backward into the snow. His body glimmered like a seashell and the woods around him seemed to sigh. Then, without a sound or any remarkable display, the light of Khors's body winked out, and in the darkness of the woods there was nothing more to be seen.

When Iris woke back up, it was the middle of the night.

Iris's heart was pounding. She had been having a nightmare. In the nightmare, she'd been standing next to Uncle Aleister's bed and Uncle Aleister had suddenly started to change. His body had gotten really, really wrinkly, and then it had turned dark and dry like coal, and then it had started to disintegrate into dust. Iris had screamed and woken herself up.

Now she looked all around her dark bedroom and then she sat up straight—she knew what she had to do.

She couldn't let Khors keep sleeping in his grave. She couldn't let him be replaced by the young God with a different name. If she woke him back up right away, maybe he wouldn't have to change at all, and then Uncle Aleister could wake up, too.

Iris slipped out of the covers and put on her slippers. She walked very, very quietly across the floor of her room and out the bedroom door, hesitating in the hallway to make sure her parents were asleep. When she was sure that they were still sleeping, she tiptoed down the stairs, keeping one hand on the railing and counting the steps as she went.

The box was still on the altar. No one had moved it. Iris had grown taller in the past year and so she could *just* reach the box. She pulled it to the edge of the bureau and carefully took it down, holding it close to her chest.

Where should she go to open it? She could take Khors back to her room—but what if her mom heard her and stopped her before she got the chance to open the box? She could turn on a light downstairs and then open the box, but again, what if her parents somehow saw the light?

Iris walked around and finally decided to open the curtains of the biggest window. After she had done this, ambient light from the street lamps as well as the moon cast just enough light for Iris to be able to see the details engraved on the box—provided she squatted down on the floor and placed the box directly in the window light.

Heart pounding, Iris opened the box. Inside, she could see Khors's statue lying just where her mom had put him. Gently, Iris reached out and picked him up.

"Hi," whispered Iris, turning the statue back and forth so she could see his face. He had a long beard, and his robe was covered with mysterious symbols. "You can get up now. It's okay. You don't have to stay asleep." Iris realized she was imitating the voice her kindergarten teacher used when one of the kids got hurt. The teacher would kneel down and put her hand on the boy or girl's shoulder, and then help the child stand up and go to the nurse. Iris was just as helpful as her teacher was. She was fixing a bad thing, allowing Khors to come back out of his grave and enjoy his life.

Iris smiled at Khors and carried him over to the coffee table, where she had him do a little dance on the slippery glass surface.

All at once there was a shuddering sound and the floor beneath Iris's knees trembled. Her stomach lurched and her heart pounded. They were having an earthquake!

But it was already over. Iris's heart was the only thing still shuddering. She got quickly to her feet, still holding the statue. Her eyes found the staircase and she was about to call out, "Mommy!" but then she realized that the light in the room was much brighter than it had been just a moment ago. Everything was illuminated with a strange green light.

Iris's turned slowly to face the window. There, as clear as the moon had just been, a hideous mottled green sun hung in the sky, its light pale and sickly. It looked as if it were rotting, like the pumpkin they had left on the porch too long after Halloween.

Iris's heart was hammering in her chest. She looked at the statue of Khors on the table. Could this have somehow happened because she took him out of his grave? Had she done something terribly wrong?

WITH A JOLT OF FIRE THAT ELECTRIFIED HIS VEINS, KHORS FOUND himself abruptly and painfully reconstituted. Every bone in his body ached as if it had been shattered and every inch of his flesh crawled as if he were covered in writhing worms. The flames that normally burned brightly and filled him with a sense of vital energy were now flickering feebly. Khors's body appeared to have rotted at the core. His decrepit old man's face was grimacing, and only two rotten teeth remained in his head. His eyes were sunk far back into his skull and peered out like two tiny lumps of coal. His normally strapping limbs were skeletal, and the flesh hung off of them in strips.

Khors's heartbeat was terribly weak and came only every

few seconds—a loud and violent *thump* that shook his rotten chest. Every breath was agony. Khors let out a loud groan and then he caught sight of Simargl, who was not far away, still hitched to the chariot, which now looked to be in the same condition as Khors; it was decrepit and emitting a sickly green light. Khors struggled to his feet, clutching his chest with one hand.

"Simargl!" he commanded. "Come here at once!"

Simargl turned to stare at Khors with eyes that were wide and terrified. The creature's nostrils flared and it bared its thousand teeth before letting out a growl, turning tail, and fleeing. As soon as the lion-dog had reached a clearing in the trees, it took off into the sky, beating its furry wings until it had disappeared from sight, still pulling the decaying green chariot behind it.

Khors let out a howl of frustration and pain. "Who has done this?" he cried out to all the creatures of the forest. "Who has brought me back in this wretched state? Show yourself! I command it!"

A great wind picked up and blew through the trees. The snow flew off the branches and the night owls hooted in alarm. Khors could feel all the creatures of the land shaking and then everything went still again.

From a long way off, Khors could hear the frantic sound of tiny footsteps as they ran back and forth. There was a pause, and then they started moving in his direction. He could hear the vibrations they made on the surface of the earth.

Whoever it was, they had responded to his command. Soon, Khors would see who was responsible.

IRIS RAN BACK AND FORTH WITH THE STATUE STILL IN HER HAND,

unsure of what to do. She put the statue back in the box and closed the lid, but the green sun didn't disappear from the sky. Iris walked around with the box in her hands, saying, "I'm sorry, Khors. I'm sorry, I'm sorry. Go back to sleep now. Pretty please?"

When she looked out the window again and saw that the green sun was still out there, she started to panic. What if her parents woke up? They had black-out curtains so they could still sleep when the sun rose, but sooner or later her dad's alarm clock would go off. What would she do then? How could she explain?

The statue was the problem. She had to get rid of it.

Iris ran to the front door and found where her coat and sweater were hanging on a hook along with her hat. She would have to get dressed all by herself, without any help. The coat would be the hardest. Iris looked back and forth just in case someone was watching, and then she crawled up onto the bench underneath the coat hooks and stood up on top of the bench very carefully, so she wouldn't lose her balance. Then she reached up and pulled down her sweater, her coat, her hat, and her scarf. She threw them to the floor and then carefully got back down off the bench, putting on her sweater first and then her coat. It took her a while to get both of her arms into her coat, and then she had to zip it up. Her mom always did that part for her because the zipper liked to get stuck.

Finally, Iris was dressed for the cold. She went to the entryway, unlocked the lock, fumbled with the slippery doorknob, and opened the door only to be greeted by a blast of icy air right in her face and the sight of her street filled with the nauseating green light. It seemed to communicate no warmth but looked heavy and diseased. Even the normally beautiful snow-covered trees looked as if they had fallen ill.

Iris shivered and looked up and down the block. If she went left, she knew, she could take the road all the way to where it met the forest. That was where she and her parents normally went for a walk every Solstice morning. It was far away, and she shouldn't go that far on her own, but right now Iris didn't have a choice.

As if hypnotized, Iris found herself turning in that direction. With Khors's box tucked securely under one arm, Iris started running up the street. As she ran, she realized it was raining, but almost as soon as she realized it, the rain stopped. Then a flock of birds filled the air overhead—hundreds of tiny, warbling birds that started to fly in one direction, then paused, hovering in a great cloud in the air before starting to go in another direction, then pausing again.

Their confused calling-out made Iris's heart pound. She stopped and squinted up at them, calling out, "Go away, birds! Go away!" She waved at them with her free arm that wasn't holding the box. Finally, the birds seemed to listen to her and left, but another flock of birds appeared as soon as the first had gone, and then the trees that lined the road began to fill with chattering squirrels. The high-pitched sound made the back of the hair on the back of Iris's neck stand up. Then, dozens of tiny objects began to fall from the trees. Iris didn't realize what they were until one of them hit her on the head. "Ow!" she yelled, rubbing the tender spot. The object bounced to the ground in front of her and she saw the familiar shape of an acorn. The squirrels were throwing away all of their winter food.

"Stop!" Iris called at them, pausing again to turn and talk to the squirrels. "You need that food! It's still winter!"

But the squirrels didn't listen and only chattered louder. The acorns were starting to pile up at the sides of the street.

Iris realized she needed to hurry. She started running again, as fast as she could.

Somehow, Iris made it all the way to the forest without stopping any more times or even slowing down to a walk. It was the longest and farthest she'd ever run. She wished her mom and dad could have been there to see it. Iris's side hurt and she was breathing really hard, but she went past the trail entrance and started down the familiar path.

Iris scanned the forest around her for a suitable place to dispose of Khors. For some reason, even though she was under the cover of trees, the green light hadn't gone away. If anything, it seemed to have gotten brighter.

Iris had gone only a short way down the path before she got so scared that she started to feel sick. She should just bury the box quick, she thought, and then get out of there.

To her right, she saw what looked like the tracks of a sled going off through an opening between the trees. Iris wanted to turn around, but she found herself following these tracks forward. It seemed like they were leading her to somewhere she needed to go, maybe a place to bury the box.

Iris reached a small clearing, entered it, and then she stopped. From the edge of the trees she felt like something was watching her, but she couldn't see what. When she looked in that direction all she saw was the green glow. It was bright enough there to hurt her eyes.

She knelt to the ground and began digging a hole through the snow with her hands. The snow was cold and firm and it was hard to dig very deep. Her fingers felt like they were starting to freeze and she tried to use the edge of the box to bang her way through the snow and make the hole deeper.

Iris had only managed to shove the box about halfway into the ground before all of a sudden she felt like she *had* to run.

Iris stood up, eyes on the trees where she had felt something watching her. All she could see was the green light, but it seemed to be getting closer. She left the box where it was and turned around and ran in the other direction as fast as she could.

She ran out of the forest and down the road, passing the frantic squirrels and the flocks of birds, and she didn't stop running until she arrived at her doorstep. Then, panting, tired and scared, Iris looked up at her front door only to realize that someone was standing right on the porch, waiting for her. Smiling. Her heart soared.

It was her Uncle Aleister.

"UNCLE ALEISTER?" SAID IRIS.

She had been certain it was him, but it was hard to tell in the green light.

"How's my little Iris?" asked Uncle Aleister, opening his arms in a familiar gesture that made Iris bound up the steps to reach him. When Iris reached the top stair, Uncle Aleister swept her up into a hug, picking her up off the ground so that her legs kicked in the air. She shrieked and then laughed as her fear dissolved into relief. She wrapped her arms around her uncle and buried her face in his puffy coat. His fluffy black beard tickled her forehead, and he smelled like she remembered: warm and a little bit like apple pie.

Uncle Aleister set her back down and then he opened the door.

"Shall we go inside?"

Iris nodded and took his hand as they went in.

"Don't turn on the lights!" Iris warned her uncle in a whisper when he reached for the switches and started flicking them on. "Someone will wake up!" Iris looked toward the stairs, listening for the sound of footsteps. Her mom almost always woke up whenever Iris did anything, even if she only wanted to go pee, and then her mom would say, *What are you doing awake? Isn't it time for bed?*

"Not to worry," said Uncle Aleister, winking. "I don't think anything could wake them up now. Do you know what time it is?"

"No."

"That's because it isn't any time."

Iris stared at her uncle, trying to figure out if he was joking. "Huh?" she said at last. "That doesn't make any sense."

"Yes, it does," said Uncle Aleister, and he spun in a little circle, kind of like a ballerina. "Normally, time is about movement and change. It's cyclic—that means, it moves in a circle. But something has happened to stop the cycle from repeating. That's why I'm able to come and visit you like this."

"Oh. Well... that's good, I guess."

"The only problem," said Uncle Aleister, his arms drooping back down to the sides, "is that I'm so very tired. But I can't fall back asleep."

"But you were already sleeping for a really long time!" Iris pointed out. "So how can you still be tired?"

Uncle Aleister thought for a moment. He did actually look pretty tired, Iris thought. Then he said, "Do you know how a car needs gas in it to run, and if it runs out of gas, it won't go any farther? I guess I'm like a car that has run out of gas. I just can't keep going, no matter how much I might want to."

"But isn't there any way to fix it?"

Uncle Aleister smiled. "But I don't need fixing."

"You do!" said Iris. "You're broken. Aren't you? That's why you can't get up. So someone needs to fix you."

Uncle Aleister shook his head. He was still smiling. "Sometimes, when something breaks, you just need to let it go."

"But I'll never let you go!" Iris cried, rushing toward Uncle Aleister and wrapping her arms around him. "Never, never, never!"

Uncle Aleister wrapped his arms around Iris, stroking her hair, and waited until she pulled back and looked up at him.

"My sweet little Iris. I'm so lucky to have you. But we can't stay like this forever, can we?"

"Why not?"

Iris looked around the room. With the lights in the house on, the green light from outside wasn't as strong. They could shut the curtains and they could live together like this, couldn't they? What was stopping them? They could keep things just like they were.

"Go upstairs and check on your parents. Then you'll see."

"You want me to wake them up?"

"Just go see."

Iris reluctantly let go of her Uncle Aleister and walked over to the staircase. At the bottom step she hesitated, looking back at him nervously, but Uncle Aleister gestured that she should go, and so she began climbing the stairs.

At first she went slowly, but then she went faster, smiling. Her parents would be so impressed when she woke them up! They had thought there wasn't any way for Uncle Aleister to get back up, but she'd proven them wrong!

She raced up the last few stairs and to the door of her parents' bedroom. "Wake up, wake up!" she called. "Guess who's here?"

Iris flicked on the light switch, but the lights didn't turn on. The room remained dark. She couldn't see anything.

"Wake up!" she called again, but she didn't hear any reply,

so she went to the window and threw open the curtains. Eerie green light filled the room, falling on her parents' faces. Their eyes were still closed.

Iris ran to her mom and grabbed her by the shoulder. She started to shake her. "Come on, Mom. Wake up!"

No matter how hard Iris shook her mom, however, she didn't stir.

Beginning to panic, Iris ran around to the other side, to her dad.

"Wake up, Dad! Come on! Please! Won't you wake up?"

Her dad's face remained still. His eyes were closed gently, as if he were having a pleasant dream.

Iris ran back out of the room and downstairs to where her Uncle Aleister was waiting for her.

"What's wrong with them? What happened?" she demanded.

"I told you—time's frozen. I can visit you because you called me and because I was already in the half-way place. But if time doesn't move forward, then your parents can't wake back up."

"No!" Iris cried. Tears filled her eyes. "That's not fair! Now you're back awake, but they're stuck asleep! It's not fair! It's not fair!" Iris stomped the ground with both her feet as hard as she could until Uncle Aleister came and wrapped his arms around her. She hit him on the chest but he just kept hugging her, and eventually, she put her head against him and cried.

When she was done, she wiped her eyes and looked up at him.

"I don't want my parents to stay asleep," she said.

"I don't blame you," said Uncle Aleister.

"So how do I fix it?"

"I think you'll have to undo whatever it was you did in the first place."

"The statue," said Iris, looking at the empty place on the altar. "I have to put it back where it belongs."

Her uncle nodded.

"But that means I'll have to go back to the forest..." Iris looked toward the front door, and then spun on her uncle. "And that means *you'll* have to go back to sleep again! But I don't want you to. Can't you *please* stay awake?"

"Well," said her uncle, smiling gently, "I won't go anywhere until you get back here. Okay?"

"Promise?" said Iris.

Uncle Aleister nodded. "Promise."

WHEN IRIS GOT BACK TO THE FOREST, EVERYTHING WAS DIFFERENT. The beginning of the trail was the same, but after that, everything changed. As soon as she had gone a short distance down the path, the trees and even the landscape looked different. The snow, which had previously covered everything in sight, began to melt as she walked deeper into the woods. The birdsong, which had filled the air overhead, got quiet the farther she went in until the only sound Iris could hear was that of her own breathing. The trees began to drip. Branches that had grown heavy under wet snow bent—the snow sloughed off of them and they sprang back up again, bare.

Iris wanted to turn around and run the other way, but she knew that she couldn't, not if she wanted her parents to wake back up. She had to find the statue, wherever it was she had left it. It had to be here somewhere.

But long after she should have seen the sled tracks that led to the clearing where the statue was buried, Iris was still walking, looking for anything that might tell her where she was.

By this time, the snow had completely melted and all the plants around her were green and lush. They looked even greener than normal plants because of the green light. Some of them had flowers, but the flowers were also green, their petals long and wide and glossy. As Iris continued walking, the flowers she saw kept getting bigger until they were bigger than any flowers she'd ever seen. They were the size of her head, and all of them were facing her. When she looked at them, it seemed like they were open mouths, waiting to swallow something. Iris swallowed gulped and looked away from them, keeping her eyes on the path in front of her, which was getting narrower and narrower. The plants kept getting closer all around her, the giant flowers brushing up against her on either side. They were almost kissing her face. Iris had to hold her arms up in front of her to push them out of the way as she walked past. Under her feet, the texture of the ground was changing as well—where the dirt path had been, it was like she was walking over wet, curly black wool. It looked like the stuff that had fallen off the sheep that she saw get shaved at the country fair last summer. But a whole lot of sheep must have gotten shaved in order for there to be this much wool on the ground. Iris found herself kicking her feet through it as she walked. It was lumpy and uneven. Still, she kept walking forward until the path she had been following had totally vanished.

Iris stopped. She had no way to keep going forward unless she wanted to lose herself in the woods forever.

She stood there a long time, not wanting to turn around and give up. The overwhelmingly green woods made her eyes feel funny. She kept rubbing them and blinking, as if this would turn things back to their normal color. Finally, she turned around, and on the path just behind her she saw the strangest creature she had ever seen. A scream caught in her throat but didn't come out.

The face was what she noticed first: it was that of a bear, except it had a monkey's mouth and long dangling hairy ears. The body it was attached to was that of a giant serpent. Its green coils gleamed as it shifted about on the woolly ground, but its body was so long that it trailed far off into the distant trees and Iris couldn't see where its tail actually ended.

The creature looked at her with wide, white eyes that had no pupils, though they had irises that looked like sunbeams. It didn't seem to have eyelids, since it never blinked. The creature shifted back and forth on its snake's body, never taking its eyes off of her.

This was when Iris should have woken up from the nightmare. Normally, she would have screamed, and that would have woken her up. But for some reason, her scream hadn't come out, and she was still standing here. The creature wasn't chasing her. It was just looking at her. What was it doing here, and what did it want?

"Are... you going to eat me?" Iris managed to stutter.

"My name is Veles," said the creature. "I am the guardian of the Underworld."

"So..." said Iris, trying to figure out what that meant, "you're *not* going to eat me?"

Veles gave a hiss that sounded a bit like a growl and Iris yelped and stepped backward. He *was* going to eat her! But Veles just shifted back and forth more urgently. "I'm not going to eat you. The divide between the worlds has been broken. Khors had been in my domain, resting, but someone pulled him out before he was ready. The problem is, they didn't pull him all the way, so he took part of my world with him. Now he's gone mad. He's at the foot of the World Tree, and he's changing everything. I couldn't keep him away any longer, and what he's doing... it isn't good."

"Oh?" said Iris, relieved that she wasn't going to be eaten. "Why? What's Khors doing?"

Veles's voice rose louder, and he sounded more like a bear as he spoke. "Corrupting the Underworld, and the Overworld with it! Things that were dead are becoming alive, and things that were alive are becoming dead. Soon, there won't be any difference between the two, and everything will exist in a halfway state. That includes you. If you go to the World Tree, you'll see what I mean."

"I don't want that to happen to me!" said Iris. She wasn't really sure what Veles was talking about, but it sounded like something bad. She *really* shouldn't have woken Khors up.

"No one wants it to happen," said Veles. "It'll be the end of the world. No more living, no more dying."

Veles fell silent and Iris thought about what that meant. The end of the world meant that there would be no more Uncle Aleister, no more parents, and no more Iris. That was unacceptable. She wouldn't allow it.

"Okay," said Iris. "Where is Khors? He's at a tree?"

Veles gestured with his head in the direction of his tail. Iris followed it with her eyes off into the distance of the thick green woods.

"The World Tree," he said. "That's where I'm coming from. If you want to find it, then follow my tail. It will lead you to Khors. But be careful. You won't make it there fully alive."

Iris swallowed hard and tried to be brave. She wanted to run back out of the woods and go back home, but if she did that, then who was going to save them? She had to get the statue and put it back on the altar. Uncle Aleister would be waiting for her. He had promised.

"Did Khors have a statue with him?" Iris asked.

Veles's head shifted back and forth on his body as he thought.

"A statue?" he finally hissed. "I think so. But I'm not sure. I got out of there as fast as I could."

"Okay," said Iris. She would just have to hope that he did.

She took a deep breath and started to walk into the woods, following Veles's long tail. She had only taken a few steps, however, when Veles called out, "Wait!"

Iris turned.

"Take that bottle," he said, indicating an empty glass bottle lying on the forest floor. Iris hadn't noticed it before that moment. "And hold it to my lips. I'll give you some of my venom. If you can persuade Khors to drink it, it should knock him out for a little while. But be careful. He'll be extra angry when he wakes back up."

Iris took off her mittens and went and picked up the bottle from out of the wet wool. The wool felt strange against her fingers. She wiped the bottle off against her coat so it wouldn't be too slippery, and then she unscrewed the top. It still smelled strongly of alcohol.

She held the bottle to Veles's lips and he spit into the container until about an inch of liquid had collected at the bottom. Thankfully, none of his venom got on to her fingers. She was afraid it would burn.

Iris couldn't imagine why anyone would ever want to drink the bottle of venom, but she thanked Veles anyway and carefully screwed the top back on before putting the bottle in her coat pocket.

Then she followed the length of Veles's body away through the trees.

As Iris walked, she began to feel very strange. It got harder and harder to move, and she started to hear sounds in the woods all around her. They were strange, horrible sounds, like claws scrabbling against the earth. The green flowers no longer looked healthy like they had before. Their petals were wilting and curling up and they looked like they were frowning.

Iris walked quickly, sticking close to the serpent's body, but then a sound from just in front of her suddenly intensified. She saw the wool that surrounded Veles's body heave and then something burst out of the ground—Iris screamed.

It was a deer, half rotten. Its skull was totally bare, but flesh still clung to its ribs. It scrambled to stand upright and then, making a terrible sound from what remained of its throat, it hurried off through the trees.

Iris felt sick. Her heart was beating too fast. But even after she stopped feeling scared, her body still felt wrong. What was happening to her? Was she going to die?

Iris fell to her knees and started throwing up. She threw up for a long time, worse than when she'd had the flu. It made her cry and shake and a lot of stuff came out, stuff that was black and brown and red. It was like she was turning inside out, like she was losing herself. Iris's head got fuzzy and her eyes got bleary. When she finally stopped throwing up, she felt like she was much skinnier than she had been, and she had almost no energy. In order to stand back up, she had to wrap her arms around Veles's slithering body and pull herself upright. It took all the strength she had. When she got back on her feet, she was dizzy, and she had to stand there for a minute with her eyes closed.

When she opened them again, she felt that something was wrong. Everything was too quiet. Something was missing. Iris raised her hands to her chest.

Her heart had stopped beating.

Iris was so frightened she might have died from the shock, but then she realized that, too, was no longer possible. In the state she was now in, she couldn't die and she couldn't live, either. This was what Veles had meant. But there was still one thing she could do.

She had to stop Khors.

WHEN IRIS ARRIVED AT THE TIP OF VELES'S TAIL, SHE REACHED THE clearing in which the World Tree grew. By this time, Iris had become disconnected from her body. It was worse than running a temperature. Right now, she felt like she wasn't inside her body at all. It had gotten too hot and painful in there and so instead of being inside of it, she was floating above it while her body continued to move forward, like a zombie, toward her destination.

When Iris saw the World Tree, she told herself to stop. A moment later, her body stopped moving. The tree was so tall that Iris couldn't see the top of it, and its roots were so long that they extended all throughout the land. The entire trunk was covered with gigantic, wilting green flowers, and at the foot of the tree Iris got her first glimpse of the source of all this trouble.

Khors was stumbling about in front of the trunk, and compared to the tree, the God looked tiny. His limbs were decaying and his skeleton was showing through his skin, but he was glowing with the same green light that had permeated the entire forest. *That* must have been what had been watching her in the clearing. It had been Khors all along.

Iris now understood what Veles had meant when he said that Khors had gone mad. The god was talking to himself, gesturing wildly, and pointing his fingers while he yelled out commands.

Whenever he pointed in a particular direction and shouted, Iris heard the scrabbling sound of claws or hooves on dirt that meant a dead animal was heaving itself out of the earth. That must have been why the outer forest had been so quiet. Any animals that were still all the way alive must have run away.

Iris couldn't see well enough to be certain, but she thought she saw the shape of a wooden box just behind Khors, propped up against the tree's massive drunk. After she'd left the box in the woods, Khors must have stolen it!

She had to get it back. But how could she get past him?

Iris's thoughts were fuzzy. It was impossible to concentrate. It would be easier, she thought, to stop trying to think at all. Then, she could just let herself be pulled along by her body without having to make any decisions. She could stop trying to be alive.

Iris.

Out of nowhere, her Uncle Aleister's voice came to her.

Don't give up. You're strong. You can do this.

With a rush of emotion, Iris felt herself pulled back into her body. She felt in her pocket for the bottle of Veles's venom. With a great effort of will, she forced her body to walk forward into the clearing. Khors spotted her immediately. He pointed his fingers at her and shouted.

Iris felt like she'd been struck by lightning. For a second, it stopped her completely. But then she made herself keep walking.

It was like moving through something very sticky, like treading through water so thick that each step took all of her strength. Her head hurt like the air was pressing down on her from above, and in front of her Khors's decaying body kept dancing back and forth, pointing and shouting.

Eventually, Iris couldn't get any closer. She was still a long way away from the god and the tree. No matter how much she tried, she couldn't make her limbs move another inch.

What do I do? What do I do? She asked herself silently. She imagined her mom and dad in their bedroom, stuck in their beds, asleep. What would they have done?

And then she remembered the Solstice ritual, how her dad had poured the alcohol into the little glass for Khors.

Iris looked at the bottle in her hand. Wasn't this the same thing her dad had offered?

She couldn't take another step, but she had enough strength to throw the bottle.

Iris pulled her arm back and then threw it forward as hard as she could, while at the same time yelling, "Khors, drink this offering!"

The bottle flew through the sky and fell on the ground some distance from the World Tree. Khors didn't seem to notice and kept dancing and shouting, but then, just when Iris thought she had failed, Khors stopped. He looked over at the bottle and began to move toward it. He walked like an animal, his shoulders bent forward, his arms dangling, his fingers wiggling. It was terrifying.

When he reached the bottle, he paused, staring down at it. Then he reached down, picked up the bottle, unscrewed the top, and drank the liquid down quickly. Iris held her breath while she watched. Khors burped, patted his stomach, and then turned and walked back to the tree. He began to resume his wild dancing, but he had only just started when his motions slowed and then stopped completely.

Before her eyes, Khors paused. He swayed for a moment, and then he fell like a tree that had just been just chopped down.

All at once, the heaviness in the air was gone. With a great and painful lurch, Iris's heart started to beat again. She cried out from the pain of it but then she leapt forward with the sheer joy of having her body returned to her.

Knowing she didn't have long, she ran toward the fallen god. There, behind his body, against the tree, was the box.

Iris picked it up and quickly opened it to make sure that the statue was still inside.

It was.

"Thank you, Veles!" Iris said, and holding the box close to her body, she ran toward Veles's distant, retreating tail, following it back to the forested path and from there, all the way home.

THE ROTTEN GREEN SUN WAS STILL HANGING IN THE SKY, BUT THE flocks of birds were no longer hovering overhead. Instead, the entire street was deathly silent. Iris imagined all the people in the houses lying frozen in their beds just like her parents were. She shuddered and ran faster, as fast as the wind.

When Iris reached her house, she ran inside and found that the lights were still on. She went down the entrance hall and rounded the corner.

There was her Uncle Aleister, sitting on the couch. His head was hanging forward so that his chin was touching his chest, and his body appeared lifeless.

"I told you to wait!" cried Iris. She dropped the box on the floor and rushed over to him. When she grabbed her uncle's hands she felt that they were still warm. As she watched him, her uncle opened his eyes and smiled.

"There's my little Iris," said Uncle Aleister, but his voice sounded weak. Iris crawled onto the couch next to him.

"Why is the green sun still in the sky?" she asked. "Why isn't everything back to normal? I've done everything I can think of! There was a monster, and he gave me his venom, and I was almost dead... and I've done everything! What more do I have to do?"

"I'm not sure," said Uncle Aleister. "Why don't you tell me everything that's happened step by step, and then we'll see if we can figure something out."

AFTER IRIS HAD TOLD HER UNCLE ALEISTER THE WHOLE STORY IN order, he sat for a while with his eyes closed, thinking.

"It seems to me that you need to put Khors back to sleep."

"But how?"

"Well, how did your parents do it?"

"First, they put him in the box on the altar... oh. Yeah."

Iris looked over at the box where it was lying on the floor. She got up off the couch and went and picked it up, then carefully replaced it on the altar before looking expectantly out the window.

The green sun was still there.

"Did they do anything else?" asked Uncle Aleister.

"Well, they gave him a drink. And then we sang a song."

"Ah!" said Uncle Aleister, nodding. "The lullaby. No one can go to sleep without first hearing a good lullaby."

Iris looked at her uncle nervously. "But after I sing it, will you be gone?"

"I won't be all the way gone."

"What do you mean?"

"You'll see. You just have to trust me."

"But I don't want to!"

"It's okay. I'll sing the song with you. Come here and help me get up."

Uncle Aleister reached out a hand, and Iris went and took it, pulling with all her might until her uncle stood up. They walked over to the altar together, and Uncle Aleister's hand was very heavy on Iris's shoulder. He was pushing kind of hard. He must have been very tired, to lean on her like that.

"Ready?" her uncle asked, and he waited for Iris to start singing before he joined in. Iris remembered all the words and she didn't mess up, but for some reason her voice sounded funny and like it was full of tears, even though Uncle Aleister seemed fine.

When they had finished singing, nothing happened, but all of a sudden Iris grabbed her Uncle Aleister by both hands.

"I don't want you to go! I don't want you to! Please!"

Uncle Aleister was smiling, but his eyes weren't focusing all the way. He put one hand on Iris's head.

"Don't worry about me, little one. I'll leave you a sign."

Iris tried to grab him, but the lights all turned out. The green sun vanished without a trace, and the whole house went dark. At the same time, her Uncle Aleister vanished right in front of her, leaving Iris all alone downstairs.

"No!" Iris cried, and then she started to sob.

A moment later, she heard the sound of her mom waking up. There were voices—her mom and dad talking—and then her mom rushed downstairs, turning on the light and seeing Iris sitting there on the floor, shaking and crying.

"Oh, baby!" said her mom, running toward her. "Come here. What happened?"

But Iris couldn't say anything. She couldn't even get up. She just let her mom pick her up and carry her upstairs and put her back in bed, where she cried until she finally fell asleep.

AT THE FOOT OF THE WORLD TREE, KHORS HAD JUST STARTED TO wake up out of his venom-induced stupor when he heard a sweet sound coming from the distance. It was the sound of two people who loved each other. They were telling each other goodbye.

Khors heard this sound, and all at once his anger went out of him. As it left him, he found himself sinking deep into the earth, and a restful feeling filled his bones as warm darkness surrounded him. Khors sighed, and as he let go of his body he felt the woods around him start to heal as they returned to their natural state. The Underworld once again separated from the Overworld. Khors could finally rest. In the land of the living, snow began to fall.

YARILO, THE YOUNG GOD, YAWNED AND STRETCHED, AWAKENING for the first time in many months. He had dreamed of being an old God with a fiery temper, and of a young girl who had tried to interfere with the course of time.

Yarilo rubbed his eyes and looked all around him. He was deep in a forest where the snow was piled deep. How had he gotten there? He could almost remember...

"Simargl!" he called out, standing to his feet, and from out of the bushes trotted the trusty lion-dog. Hitched to the creature's back was Yarilo's chariot, and it was just beginning to glow with the light of the new sun. Yarilo could feel his energy growing by the moment. He was ready to begin his new journey around the earth.

IRIS DIDN'T WAKE UP INSTANTLY ON SOLSTICE MORNING. THE LIGHT of the sun filled the room but Iris stayed in bed. Her whole body was more tired than it had ever been and her eyes were dry and ached from having cried so much.

I won't be all the way gone. I'll leave you a sign, her uncle had said.

But what did he mean? Iris still didn't understand.

Eventually, Iris got out of bed and put on her slippers and went downstairs. Both of her parents were already awake, sitting on the couch drinking coffee. When they saw her, they smiled.

"Good morning, sweetheart!" said her mom.

"How's my little bear?" said her dad. "Happy Solstice! Hey—who's that on the altar?"

Iris walked over to the altar and saw that while she had slept her parents had put a new statue on the altar. It looked a little bit like the old one of Khors, but when she examined it closely, the details were different.

"That's Yarilo?" asked Iris. Her dad got up off the couch and came over to her.

"That's right. And now that you're awake, we can welcome him properly. Do you want some orange juice?"

"Okay."

Iris's dad went to the kitchen while her mom sat there on the couch, drinking her coffee. When her dad got back, her mom got up and they all took a glass of orange juice and held it up in the air, facing the statue.

"Yarilo, the young sun, we welcome your light. Now that we've gotten through the darkest night of the year, may you bring brightness to the days ahead."

"To Yarilo," said her mom.

"To Yarilo," Iris whispered.

She drank from her cup but the orange juice tasted sour. How could her parents be so happy to see Yarilo when Khors had only just left? Didn't they miss him at all?

"What's wrong, honey?" asked her mom.

"He's not the same!" Iris cried, and she threw her glass onto the ground where it shattered, splashing orange juice all over the floor. Shards of broken glass gleamed and in their reflection all Iris could see was her Uncle Aleister—broken and unfixable, never to get up again.

Iris didn't wait to see if her parents would be angry or not and instead ran back upstairs to her room. She didn't want the sun to rise if it was a different sun. She hated the passage of time. She wanted to turn it back.

For a few minutes, no one came upstairs, and Iris thought maybe her parents didn't care anymore. They didn't understand what it was she was feeling. They didn't know what it felt like to miss someone with your whole heart. You couldn't just put up a new statue and pretend that it was the same one. No one could ever replace Uncle Aleister; he was one of a kind.

Eventually, Iris's mom and dad came into her room. They walked very quietly, like they thought maybe she was asleep. Iris didn't move and waited until they had sat down on the bed next to her.

"Iris," said her mom, "I didn't want to have to tell you this first thing on Solstice morning, but this morning we got a call from the hospital. Your Uncle Aleister passed away in the night."

Iris closed her eyes tightly. Somehow she had known it was true. She had been hoping it wasn't, but deep in her aching heart she had felt that he was already gone.

"But," her mom continued, "he knew this was coming, and he left something that he wanted us to give to you when this happened."

Iris opened her eyes and looked up. In her mom's hands was a present. It wasn't wrapped properly but was just folded in tissue paper.

Iris took it and held it. Had last night been a dream? Or had it really happened? She couldn't be sure, and she was almost afraid to open the present and find out.

At last, however, she looked back and forth between her parents' faces, and then she unwrapped the tissue paper to reveal a small stuffed animal. It was a bear whose fur was as black as midnight except for a white patch right under its chin on its chest.

Iris hugged the bear, holding it close to her heart. It wasn't the same. But she would love it anyway.

SOLSTICE CAROL FOR KHORS, GOD OF THE OLD SUN

(Sung to the tune of "We Three Kings")

Sleep, Sweet Khors

Sleep, sweet Khors, magnificent one
God who rules the Solstice sun
All these days your name we've praised
But now your work is done

Oh, Sun of wonder, Sun so bright
Sun that gave the earth its light
You must rest, you've done your best
But now it's time to say goodnight

Sleep, Sweet Khors, the whole night through
There is nothing more to do
You were king and so we'll sing
Our children songs of you

Oh, Sun of wonder, Sun so bright
Sun that gave the earth its light
You must rest, you've done your best
But now it's time to say goodnight

With each year we all will grow old
And each night the earth will grow cold
Still we live and love and give
Our thanks to those we hold

Oh, Sun of wonder, Sun so bright
Sun that gave the earth its light
You must rest, you've done your best
But now it's time to say goodnight

SNOW ANGEL
Seven Jane

THE WINTER WIND HAD SWEPT IN A COLDER DECEMBER THAN usual, one that chilled Crystal Townsend to her bones where she stood at her kitchen window, wrapped in her fleece house robe and sipping lukewarm Earl Grey tea as she watched the bright rays of morning sun struggle to break through a frozen sky. It didn't snow in the South—at least not as part of the usual course of things—but on occasion it did frost, and the storm that had moved in overnight had far outstripped expectations of what normal winter weather was like in this part of the country. As predicted, frost had appeared, covering the dusty soil with a thin smattering of silver. Then, much to everyone's surprise, came sleet, which turned to layers of ice, and under the cover of night it had encased Crystal's backyard—and much of the surrounding landscape—in strange sheets of silvery white that seemed more alien to the season than the crusted, desiccated plants had been.

Crystal watched through the window as the layer of ice on her lawn shifted and sparkled with an almost impish sort of twinkle, as if it knew it didn't quite belong anywhere below thirty-five degrees latitude and was proud to have slipped in unnoticed. The frost hadn't arrived alone, Crystal mused, but like a wily warrior had brought with it an infantry of soft, powdery snow that was now sprinkling itself on the bark of the pine trees that edged the expanse of her small countryside property. Combined with the frost and ice, the dusting of snow covered everything in a thin layer of white, turning anything green to inky black and even giving the late morning sky the hoary feel of twilight. The trees started to look like upright Yule logs as the snow clung to their bark, all chocolate and powdered sugar and inevitable cavities, with sweet little gumdrop baubles clinging to their outer branches. Draped in their thin white dresses, the few evergreen trees and plump bushes of Crystal's well-manicured lawn were transformed into an emerging winter wonderland, reflected in the icicles that traced along the eaves of her home like icing on a gingerbread house.

After three decades of winters in the South, Crystal had never seen a morning quite as dreadful as this. She didn't like it, she decided, taking another sip of tea before recoiling at the sensation of tepid liquid on her tongue that indicated she'd need to reheat her tea—again. Crystal tightened the fabric of her robe and then refilled her mug with hot water from the kettle. At only a few days before the holiday, the skies promised a white Christmas, but to Crystal the landscape was nothing but cold, frozen, and inhospitable. Even the promise of building snowmen—something her son, Billy, had wished for every year in his annual letter to Santa—wasn't enough to warm her heart to the beauty of the first snowy morning Southeast Texas had seen in years.

It seemed so unlikely now that she had ever wished for a morning like this in her own youth, when her dreams this time of year had been filled with images of ice skating on frozen ponds or catching a glimpse of Santa and his reindeer from his perch atop a snow-covered rooftop. But she had wished for them. In fact, once—and not all that long ago—Crystal might have said that such a sight as that outside her kitchen window was beautiful, that the normally green fields blanketed in the hush of freshly fallen snow was majestic, particularly in an area that had a stubborn tendency not to drop below fifty. It would have felt renewing—transformative—and it would have catapulted her into holiday fervor. She'd have launched into a frenzy of baking, wrapping, and crafting. But this year, at barely thirty degrees, the frozen morning wasn't beautiful, and no amount of cheer would be enough to lift her bankrupt spirit. Not this year, and not last, nor the year before, for that matter, and none of those had even dared to dip below sweater weather.

It hadn't always been this way. There had been a time when she had loved this season—the cookies, the gifts, the bustling shopping spaces and tunes on every radio wave. Now it was the time of year she dreaded most, and for all of the same reasons. The holiday season felt hollow after you grew up and lost sight of the magic that had animated everything when you were too young to know better—when holiday characters like Ebenezer Scrooge and Seuss's Grinch seemed so unreasonable. Crystal had become far more sympathetic to those stressed-out old misers of late until, at last, she'd come to find herself agreeing with their bah humbugs.

Christmas, she now believed, wasn't cookies and bows and good cheer; it was garbage and extra calories and stress. She'd tried her best to get into the spirit, but the errands and to-do lists and unnecessary hustle and bustle all for the sake of fulfilling some Currier and Ives ideal had worn her down. Instead of sugarplum visions, her sleep had become filled with nightmares of exorbitant holiday bills and calendars overstuffed with too many holiday commitments, all tinged with the stench of flocked Christmas trees and burnt sugar.

If there'd ever been more to the holidays than stress and frustration, shiny packaging and rabid consumerism, Crystal had long forgotten what it was. Much like her iced-over backyard, the place inside her heart that had previously flickered with the heat of the holiday spirit had grown hollow and cold.

I must stop Christmas from coming, Crystal reflected, quoting the famous line in her head for what must easily have been the millionth time that week. If only such a thing were possible. Crystal's eyes tracked the movement of a fresh batch of snowflakes as they floated lazily down from the swirling gray overhead.

With a heavy inhale of the rich bergamot aroma of her tea, she wondered idly if her roses would return in warmer weather. Probably not, she thought. Frozen things didn't spring back to life easily, not without copious amounts of care and nurturing, and sometimes not even then. Cold had a way of ending things, of halting life in mid-motion and hardening it, turning it to stone from the inside out so completely that it left no trace of what had been there before. Even when—*if*—they thawed, such frozen things rarely returned unchanged. Crystal scoffed into the steam rising from her mug as the flakes alighted on the outstretched fingers of the dusty pine that reached upward, the branches as eager as children to catch the fragile flakes on their fingertips. It was so easy for some to embrace the curiosity of the cold—glittering frost, sprinkling snow—without considering what it meant to freeze.

As silly as it seemed, Crystal couldn't shake the feeling that the cold outside was an extension of that inside her, as if the chill that lingered beneath her skin had managed to seep out and was starting to impact the world outside her door. What was awakening outside didn't feel like the kind of white-speckled winter's morn one would find stamped on any of the dozen or so Christmas cards collecting in unopened heaps on Crystal's kitchen counter. It seemed tempered with a different kind of chill, something sharper and more unforgiving. The holidays would arrive soon and, at least to Crystal, it seemed very possible that by the time they did, she might be as irreparably frozen as her rose bushes.

Crystal sensed movement behind her.

"Still the Ice Age outside?" asked a deep voice as Crystal's husband wrapped his arms around her. Clark set his chin atop her head, his warmth sliding over Crystal's shoulders as he pressed his body against her back. He squeezed her against him, and the unshaven stubble—the kind he only grew when he was on vacation and didn't have to shave—passed with rough reassurance over Crystal's cheek.

"Baby, it's cold outside," Clark sang in mock frivolity, his hands sliding into the pockets of her robe.

In spite of herself, Crystal softened in her husband's embrace. Of all of Clark's good qualities—of which there were a considerable few—his voice, especially when he sang, was one of the things she loved most. It was heat against cold, tenderness against harshness, and more comforting than any instrumental hymn on a lonely winter's night. Just hearing her husband's voice now made the chill furling in Crystal's veins thaw just a little, what was still green inside her spring back just a tiny bit.

"Snowmaggedon," she confirmed, leaning into Clark's embrace. She lifted the mug to her lips and grimaced at the unwelcome coolness of the tea on her tongue as she took another sip. Her mug had gone cold again.

"Doesn't take much in these parts," he agreed. "A little bit of frost on the windshield in the morning might as well be a blizzard. I imagine this much will shut the town down for a few days. At least it's almost Christmas, right? Who knows how long it's been since they've had snow for the holidays in Southeast Texas. It's some kind of miracle."

He was right. By Texas standards, a fingernail-thick layer of ice on the roads was not only unusual; it was enough to necessitate a complete unraveling of the local fabric. Even the threat of uncharacteristically frigid temperatures had been all it took to make the local news reporters enthusiastically declare the current weather a state of emergency. Before the sun had even set the previous day, schoolchildren had already been gifted a few extra days of winter break. Highway on-ramps were cautiously cordoned off and every business that could get away with it had flipped the signs on their doors to *Closed* with paper signs that promised a swift reopening "post-storm." Even the government offices had taken their leave, wishing patrons a happy holiday and promising they'd be back when New Year's had passed and the ice had thawed, and hoping anyone who might have official business over the holiday would understand the delay. This year at least, it looked like the holidays were starting early—but while everyone else seemed to be celebrating, the only thing Crystal could think of was all the stuff she had to get done before the big day, and how much harder a surprise snowstorm was going to make it.

"Well," Clark mused, breaking away from the holiday tune he'd been humming in an attempt to coax his wife out of her self-induced hibernation, "at least we get more vacation time out of it. It's nice for us all to be home together. I was thinking Billy and I might do some wrapping, or bust out the craft box—probably got enough stuff in there to redecorate the house ten times over. What do you think?" He busied about in the kitchen, retrieving all the ingredients for a pancake breakfast.

"I think we already have enough crafts around here to last us a lifetime," Crystal said evenly, trying not to think about all the holiday knick-knackery already cluttering up her home. The thought of pulling out all those boxes and ribbons and bows almost made her sick to her stomach. For every store-bought decoration, Billy had constructed two handprint ornaments, clay snowmen, or toilet paper Christmas wreaths to add to the holiday bulk.

"That stuff is worth its weight in gold," Clark countered. "Besides, we'd better do it now—it won't be long before Billy would rather shut himself up in his room than hang out and coat the kitchen floor in glitter making snowflakes."

Just the thought of glitter caused Crystal's anxiety to flare. On the heels of this thought, the day's schedule queued up in her mind, producing a list of errands that would be all but impossible to achieve with the day's weather. "I was supposed to go shopping this afternoon," she said, not even trying to hide the frustration in her voice as her eyes moved again to the window and the falling snow outside. It was coming down thicker now. "There are presents in the backseat of my car that need to be dropped off at the senior center, and I need to pick up some things at the grocery to finish the baking so the goody baskets can go out to Billy's Cub Scout troop. There are also packages and a box of overdue Christmas cards to mail, and no one has picked up the guest bedroom quilt from the dry cleaners—we need to get the spare room together before your parents arrive. I don't have time for crafts."

Clark turned to wave a batter-coated spatula in Crystal's direction. "Don't worry about any of that. Everything is going to be closed today anyway. Just relax. Try to enjoy the holiday, not work it. That stuff will get done or it won't—but who cares? There's more to Christmas than a perfect holiday."

Crystal scoffed, suddenly feeling very brittle in her chair. "You sound like a Hallmark movie."

"You haven't seen nothin' yet. Just wait till I get you under the mistletoe." Clark winked, returning to the pancakes bubbling on the griddle.

Crystal's smile was thin. That was easy for Clark to say. Clark, who wasn't charged with preparing the house for the arrival of family from out of town—particularly her mother-in-law, who wouldn't mince words of judgment if the sheets weren't crisp and the guest bathroom not prepared with decorative little soaps. Clark, who hadn't had to run to seven different department stores and three grocery markets to buy presents and the makings of the holiday feast for six. Who wouldn't have to wrap those presents and get them under the tree, or cook and serve that feast to perfection. Clark, who hadn't handwritten more than two hundred Christmas cards, licked them sealed, stamped them, and packed them all in the backseat of the car to be dropped off at the post office. Who wasn't in charge of Secret Santa in his office, or committed to serving as the homeroom parent in Billy's third-grade class winter party—both of which would now inevitably be reinterpreted as New Year's parties and have to be re-themed.

"I don't have time for mistletoe, Clark. If I don't work it, Christmas doesn't come. Do you think all the magic just happens?" Crystal pursed her lips in consternation. Her husband would undoubtedly try to coax her into staying home, but when everything fell apart, she would be the one to blame when Billy's eyes filled with disappointment over uncooked treats and shoddily wrapped gifts. Crystal rubbed her hands up and down her arms to generate some heat and tried to summon up a plan of attack. The smaller stores might be closed, but the large box stores would probably still be open.

The post office had a self-service kiosk. She wouldn't be able to pick up the dry cleaning, but it would be easy enough to drop off the donations at the senior center.

"So that's a no on Hallmark movies and crafts?" Clark flipped a pancake with his back to her, and Crystal thought she could hear a slight chill in his voice now as well.

"Christmas isn't a holiday anymore. It's a job. There's too much to do, and if it doesn't get done, everything falls apart."

Clark managed to flip a pancake and shrug in the same motion, apparently deciding the ensuing argument wasn't worth it. After a decade of marriage, Crystal assumed her husband had learned that when she'd made up her mind about something, it was nearly impossible to get her to change it. "Well, you're going to have a tough time of getting anything done today, Crys. I know it's not exactly Alaska out there, but you know how the roads around here are on a good day. News says they've closed the highway—overpasses are iced over. It'll be all back roads into town, and who knows what it's like there. It's not like anyone around here has a plow."

Crystal pulled her hair through her fingers without bothering to notice that her naturally dark hair seemed to have lightened to an even ashier shade of brown. Her thoughts were on her to-do list and the litany of things that she needed to accomplish to survive the season. Without highway access, getting from her house to the town center would be challenging, if not impossible. Growing up in the South and never seeing a single flurry, she'd always thought those *Beware of Ice on Bridges* signs were some sort of sarcastic joke, but now realized they were actually a big *Get the hell off the road* warning sign to the general driving public. With the overpasses down, it would mean driving at least twenty miles out of the way through old unpaved winding roads that were probably in just as bad shape as the main thoroughfares. If more sleet fell this afternoon, what would have been a two-hour excursion could take all day, and that was *if* she was able to do even a few items on her list.

Clark smoothed a thick slab of butter between two hot pancakes, drizzled a dollop of maple syrup over the top, and set the plate at the edge of the counter just as a sand-colored mop on two lanky legs bounded into the kitchen, scooped up the dish, and scampered away. Billy. The kid scarfed down food like a nocturnal critter on the prowl: dart in, snatch what you want, dart out, and leave the mess behind for someone to find later. He'd always been like that—quick, elusive, independent. He'd grown so much in the past couple years, but then again, that was to be expected. He was in third grade now and starting to become his own little person. He was bright and spirited and loved this time of year more than anything else. Then again, what kid didn't? Crystal wanted to make sure his Christmas was the best it possibly could be, and if that meant braving the Southern version of a snowstorm to make sure she had molasses for fresh gingerbread cookies—Billy's favorite—then that was what she'd do. This thought was the first warm one she'd had all morning.

"Morning, Billy Goat," Crystal called to her son's backside as it disappeared into the living room. She could see from his profile that a forkful of dripping pancakes was already on its way to his lips.

"Good morning, Mom." Billy's voice, a higher version of his dad's and thick with syrup, called back from the depths of the living room. Crystal heard the plunk of his body on the leather sofa and then the click of the TV as it spilled sounds of *Frosty the Snowman* through the rest of the house. Billy loved the old classic holiday cartoons most of all and would watch them on repeat all year if anyone would let him. He laughed on cue when one of the schoolchildren suggested they name the snowman Oatmeal.

The cold and silence of the morning seemed to thaw just a bit as Crystal's house came to life around her. Clark washed up in the kitchen and Billy giggled loudly in the living room while Crystal took another long look at the dense gray sky outside and did her best to erase the gloomy thoughts out of her mind. By the time she tore her eyes away from the cold outside, a bright flash of colorful light gave the room a warm glow. Someone—Billy, most likely—had plugged in the Christmas tree in the living room, and its twinkling blue, red, and orange lights added a festive air to the room as Crystal heard the click of the heater kick on and begin to pipe hot air through the house's vents. For a minute, Crystal almost forgot about her list of holiday chores, and it seemed like she might be able to find some joy in the season after all.

"Well, it's still early," she remarked, twisting a bite of Clark's pancakes and trying to sound more hopeful than she felt. A thin ray of clear blue light slipped through a fracture in the clouds. Maybe that was a good omen. "Maybe I can get everything done and find some time to wrap with you guys when I get back." Crystal took a deep breath. "Maybe I can do it all."

DENYING ALL CONVENTIONS OF SOUTHERN WEATHER, THE SNOW continued to fall and the land outside grew thick with frost and ice until there was a heavy coating of white as far as the eye could see. By the time Crystal had showered and dressed and gathered all of her grocery lists and packing slips the wintry haze outside was almost as prickly and unpleasant as

Crystal's attitude. She tried to remain positive, but with every falling snowflake her mood soured. By the time she kissed Billy goodbye and gave him a squeeze, Crystal made the most miserable of holiday characters seem positively cheerful.

Crystal tugged on her best winter boots, which were nothing more than thick rain galoshes lined with heavy woolen socks. She shivered inside her down coat and gloves, still unable to shake the chill that clung to her bones as she pulled a fleece beanie over her head. Winter weather gear was pretty much nonexistent in this area, so Crystal was astutely aware how underdressed she was going out into the frozen version of her hometown, but desperate times called for desperate measures. Somehow, though, she felt even colder being underdressed, as if her body knew how defenseless it would be against the chill outside.

As Crystal made her way through the bramble of empty holiday storage containers still scattered helter-skelter in her garage, Clark grabbed her arm. "Are you sure you want to go out in that?" he asked, a tone of concern in his voice. "The weather is nasty. Seriously, everything can wait. Come back in and let's enjoy the day as a family. Billy won't notice the lack of gingerbread and the cards can wait another day—we've still got a few days before Christmas. It's dangerous out there. I'd much rather you stay home with us."

Unmoved, Crystal shook her head and shivered again. "I'm sure it looks worse than it is. It's just a little bit of snow, really. I'm sure it just seems worse because we're not used to seeing it. And I have to get this stuff done." She thought again of the laundry list of chores upon which the success of the impending holiday depended, then gave her husband a light peck on the cheek and pulled her arm from his grasp. "This is what Christmas is all about, right?" she teased half-heartedly as she slid down into the driver's seat, shuffling a stray stack of unmailed Christmas cards out of her way as she did. "Santa's got his sleigh and I've got mine."

OTHER THAN HERS, THERE WASN'T A SINGLE CAR ON THE ROAD. AND Clark had been right: the roads were awful—not impassable, but certainly bad enough that anyone who could avoid going out would. No one in this area would own a snow plow to clear the roads, and it was unlikely that even the local municipality had so much as a bag of salt waiting for a snowy day that was, statistically, about as likely as everyone in the town winning the lottery at the exact same time. It was every man for himself out on the icy pavement today, or—as Crystal thought, laughing dryly to herself—every *woman*.

Crystal drove in silence, wincing at the crunch of snow and ice under her tires as she crept carefully out of her neighborhood and toward the main interstate. She didn't have tire chains, much less snow tires, and she didn't want to move too fast for fear of sliding or spinning out. She turned her heated seats on—probably the first time she'd used those since she got the car—and cranked the heat and defrost up to full blast. None of it mattered, though. Crystal was just as cold inside her car as she might have been outside, her thoughts just as bleary, and neither her seat nor her steering wheel could so much as make a dent in that.

The storm was definitely worsening, too. The snowflakes were coming down in clumps now, no longer the delicate little flakes that had earlier rested on the outstretched tips of the waiting pine branches but thick gobs of white, heavy and dense, like mini marshmallows plummeting from the sky. Sunlight had never fully managed to break through the clouds, so the day was shadowed in permanent twilight, which might have seemed cozy to some but just seemed foreboding to Crystal, as if it heralded the arrival of something darker than would normally be allowed this time of year. Today was the shortest day of the year, after all, and it would appear that even the few scant hours of daylight weren't going to have their chance to separate night from night.

As she approached the interstate, Crystal was not at all surprised to see the *Do Not Enter, Ramp Closed* sign that cordoned off the on-ramp to the highway that bridged her small suburb to the rest of town. The overpass was likely too dangerous to be crossed safely. Crystal had expected this delay. She'd never been particularly fond of bridges anyway, and so for once she didn't mind taking the back roads into town, even if it meant the fifteen-mile stretch would now become even more unnecessarily long and painstakingly tedious to navigate.

With a sigh, Crystal settled deeper into her seat and twisted the knob on the stereo, trying to find a station playing something other than carols as she wound her way through the back country roads. There weren't many options, not unless she was willing to listen to voices on news radio, haughtily instructing drivers to stay off the roads, or radio evangelists, who were preaching an equally obnoxious message about the "true meaning of the holidays."

"Baby, it's cold outside," one radio DJ said cheekily over a jingle-bell sound effect. "Might want to snuggle up by the fire and stay warm today, folks. Even Santa wouldn't go out in this mess."

"Jesus is the reason for the season," another voice drawled from the Christian radio station at the next stop on the radio, right before launching into the inevitable invitation to come, pray, and tithe. "St. Jude's on Dowlen Road will be open for Midnight mass—"

Crystal flicked the radio off and returned to silence as the snow continued to fall faster and thicker. It was getting a little challenging to see clearly, the frost crawling over her windshield almost as quickly as she could melt it, and her car's slick city tires were having a difficult time maintaining their grip on the icy road. Her car's heater didn't seem to be working, either, and the press of leather was cold on her back despite the thick layers of coats and sweaters Crystal had draped herself in. The shiny black interior of her car seemed flecked with ice crystals and her knuckles around the steering wheel were as white from her grip as they were from the cold. She sniffed and her resulting exhale billowed in front of her in the small interior space, hanging like grisly white smoke in her car's cabin.

The speedometer was hovering just below the five-mile-per-hour mark and Crystal had just entered the last stretch of her drive when a dark blur flashed suddenly across the nose of her car. It could just as easily have been a tree as a deer, but it was wider than a tree and larger than any deer she'd ever seen, even on these old roads that sliced through the edges of a national preserve. Instinctively, she stomped her foot on the brake pedal and immediately felt the car go sideways as it slid out on the frozen pavement.

She spun once, then twice, each time skidding right toward the tree line that waited just on the side of the road. Crystal screamed in fright, and just as the car was making its third rotation, the driver's side slammed into something hard and unseen, causing an abrupt stop. Her head hit the window, a curious sound of sleigh bells jingled in her ears, and then everything faded instantly to black.

THE SOUND OF HER BLINKERS TICKED IN CRYSTAL'S EARS, SNICKING like an old record player whose needle had wound its way to the end of the vinyl, when she finally opened her eyes. The nose of her car was tucked into a thick bank of snow that seemed too high and dense to have accumulated from the flurries that had been falling since morning. Rubbing her eyes and groaning against the sharp pain in her head, Crystal looked at the landscape around her as she used her windshield wipers to clear as much snow from her line of sight as she could. The battery in her car still worked and the lights still came on, but the radio was garbled and the clock on the dashboard had managed to reset itself, insisting that it was just after midnight—more than ten hours since she'd left home. The sky had grown darker, but there was an ethereal purplish hue to the night that could just as easily have been predawn or dusk, or perhaps neither, given that the light from an unseen moon reflected so brightly off the snow. She turned the blinkers and wipers off, then pushed the button to silence the radio. The resulting silence was dense and total, as if Crystal had dunked her head underwater.

"You've got to be kidding me," Crystal groaned to no one in particular, the sound of her own voice loud and abrupt in the heavy quiet. What had run out in front of her? Had that been bells she'd heard?

Crystal peered through the small clearing in her windshield that had already become mullioned with ice prisms. She didn't recognize the area. In fact, if she hadn't known she'd been driving the country back roads that surrounded her own home, she would have wondered if she was a different place altogether. The land around her certainly didn't look like Southeast Texas—it looked more like a true winter forest, the kind you'd find somewhere up north, probably in a different country.

There was no sign of whatever had raced in front of her car. Whatever it was, she hadn't hit it, and any tracks or footprints were long covered by falling snow.

Crystal shoved the gifts and cards that had scattered around the passenger seat of her car to the floorboard and dug her cell phone from the pocket of her bag. She looked at the screen—a snap of Clark and Billy during last year's summer vacation, both wearing swimming trunks and wide, goofy grins as they stood on a sandy beach—and loosed a disappointed sigh. Not a single bar. No cell service meant she couldn't call a tow or check in with her family. She wondered if they were worried about her.

"Damn," she cursed, tossing her phone back in her purse as she tried to decide what to do. It wasn't a long exercise. She had two choices: she could stay here and wait for help, or she could go out and look for it on her own.

She might have chosen the former, but with her apparent broken heater and less than ideal supplies, the idea of sitting in her car did not bring any comfort. Besides, with the weather this bad, it could be hours before Clark called anyone for help and even longer before anyone—who would be as ill-prepared as Crystal had been—would go out looking. By then, she might well and truly be irreversibly frozen. So Crystal gathered up her things, adjusted the edges of her pitifully inadequate gloves and scarf and hat, and prepared to go out into the dark winter storm on foot.

CRYSTAL STOOD BESIDE HER CAR, BUNDLED HER MEAGER GARments around her, and tried to adjust to the new sensation of feeling frozen from the inside out. The temperature gauge on her dash had still said it was thirty-one degrees outside, but considering she could already feel the wetness of her eyes beginning to freeze over, Crystal assumed that the thermometer, like the clock, had been compromised by her crash.

Apparently, she was going into this blind—both in the literal sense and the figurative one. It was impossible to tell where she was. Any landmark that might have given her a concrete idea of where she had ended up was gone, almost as if she'd crashed her car into a snow bank at the North Pole rather than the sprawling countryside of her local area. Of course, that was unreasonable. Still, there were no fields or farmhouses in view and as Crystal spun around trying to get her bearings, she saw nothing but the small alcove she'd crashed into, surrounded in all directions by dense forest buried in thick snow. She could no longer even clearly make out the road she'd traveled in on.

With every passing minute, the storm grew worse, like it was building up to some meteorological climax. Around her, the world was cast in the glowing white darkness of a twilit forest swathed in freshly fallen snow. Thick flakes floated down from the sky in slow motion, adhering as they fell to the branches of the spruce trees that punctuated their fall. Shadowy shapes of evergreens dominated the landscape—what must have been pine, fir, hemlock, and cedar—all reaching their bristle-brush arms to the moon that kept watch above them. Small or large, their branches were lazy in their stretch, all weighed down by heavy outlines of snow that traced their dendritic growth. In the deepening dark, with any signs of color camouflaged in shadow, bushy arms clothed in white reached from under their white gowns and powdered the sleeves of Crystal's jacket and shoulders as she brushed them aside to move farther into the forest.

For a moment she hesitated, but then there was something—an echo of the strange, jingling-bell-like sound she'd heard before she crashed—far off in the distance ahead of her. She turned, seeing nothing behind her but more forest, and decided to keep going straight. Even though it seemed unlikely, it appeared the only way she was going to get out of this was to go through it—toward the source of the sound and, hopefully, civilization.

The sky visible through the treetops was clouded, but sparsely so, the darkness overhead was blotted by wraith-like wisps of smoky white that hung ominously over Crystal's head. On the ground, the pathway between the trees the way was clear, lit by the ghostly whiteness of moonlight on snow. The dark made the night even colder, and Crystal shivered down to her core as she desperately rubbed her hands together for the heat of friction. She did not miss how strangely quiet the land was as she crept farther into the woods. The snowfall muted everything so that the only sound she could hear was the noise of her own footsteps compressing the loose fresh crystals of powdered snow beneath her feet. Nothing stirred in this languid land; vertebrate life dreamed the dreams of torpor. Somewhere, far off in the distance, Crystal thought she heard the sound of bells again, but it could just as easily have been tinnitus, a leftover ringing in her ears from the accident. Still, she walked onward, sucking her lips inside her mouth to keep them from cracking.

Crystal wasn't used to the awkward, stumbling walk required in what had to be at least a foot of snow. She had to walk with her legs spread slightly farther apart than her natural gait, and she struggled to keep her balance against the heavy lift of snow-laden feet. After a few difficult steps, Crystal stopped for a moment to catch her breath. The air was crisp and her lungs filled with cold, making it painful to breathe, as if a thousand tiny shards of ice swirled down her throat. She could see the mist from her labored breathing, white clouds projecting from her mouth with each exhale and dissipating some ways off, vapor condensing into tiny droplets of water and ice upon contact with the frigid air. It hurt just as badly to exhale as it did to inhale, and she had already begun to lose feeling in her fingers and toes.

She looked around. The threat of frostbite was very real.

She tried to see the beauty in the winter landscape. She tried to find the heat of the holiday spirit that had to still dwell somewhere within her—anything that would add a spark to combat the terrible cold and help her keep moving. Her thoughts turned to when she had loved Christmas and the promise of snow above anything else, her mind drifting back to her childhood.

Crystal blinked snowflakes out of her eyes and tried to reinvent the stark landscape around her to resemble the holiday wonderland her father had annually transformed her family's home into every Christmas. She fondly remembered weekends spent stringing lights with her father outside as he decked every eave and window of the family home with bright bulbs. She tried to see their colors in the space between the frozen trees.

In her memory, she could see her dad—in layers of flannel and denim as he climbed the A-frame ladder onto the roof—stapling wires down, replacing bulbs, and occasionally calling out a request for more lights, or maybe cocoa if the craving arose. Her father had approached decorating the house's exterior for the holidays with the focused precision of a baker decorating a wedding cake. A string of lights ran the perimeter of the yard, stapled to alternating red and green stakes, and a tall, slender pine tree in the corner where the driveway met the street was spiraled with alternating red and white mini-lights ten feet up, resembling a candy cane. Nearly parallel lights served as a Dickensian street, zigzagging into a vanishing point beyond a group of illuminated Victorian carolers fitted with speakers her father had rigged, their cords running from the house to pipe through Christmas music. Above, attached to the sloping roof, was the apex of her father's display, and Crystal's personal favorite: Santa and his reindeer floating above the house, hoisted up by a system of taut metal wires connected to a tree on the opposite side of the yard. It had begun with just Santa in his sleigh, waving, and a single reindeer, but he'd added a reindeer a year until the entire team had been assembled. He'd even let Crystal paint Rudolph's red nose.

Despite her best efforts at conjuring up that old vision, the night was still stark and cold and white as Crystal stared into it, unable to muster up even a single twinkle of that old house. She hadn't even been to her parents' home this year, nor had she asked if her father would be bringing out the decorations. He'd stopped at some point, passing the torch on to Clark, and Crystal had always worried too much over damage to shingles to allow him to do much more than pin a meandering strand of plain white bulbs around the outermost edge of their home. Rudolph and his chipped red nose had taken up residence in her garage, and she had no idea if his thin plastic shell had survived the summer's heat.

With as shallow a sigh as she could manage, Crystal resumed her trek. As she walked on she wondered, briefly, what Clark and Billy were up to, back at home. Maybe they'd done some wrapping, or perhaps they'd broken out the craft box after all. Crafts had been a staple of holiday festivities when she'd been growing up, and she had never been able to decide if baking with her mother or cutting paper snowflakes from large white swathes of felt and construction paper with her grandmother had been more fun.

Crystal's grandparents had lived so far away that the annual trip home for the holidays had been something of a reunion, and enough to keep the house brimming with family for the season. Rooms were swapped, bathrooms were cluttered, and there was always too much food on the table in preparation for a nightly family feast. Nana and Pawpaw usually arrived in mid to late December, and their arrival, more than anything else, always marked the moment when the holidays truly began for Crystal. Preparing for her grandparents was almost as exciting as the traditions involved with their visit—baking and singing at the piano and playing card games while old holiday movies played in the background. It was hard to leave home when they were there, and it was rarely ever necessary except for last minute trips to the mall to people-watch, or to the market for another bag of sugar. The inside of the house was just as colorful as the outside, too, with lights strung around thresholds, walls covered in a variety of quirky stockings, and a massive tree trimmed with an impossible number of twinkling bulbs and ornaments, some going back several generations and many crafted by Crystal herself.

Crystal felt a twinge of sadness over the thought of her grandmother and the old traditions she had so enjoyed. Nana had passed away when Billy was just a baby, and many of the family's traditions had gone with her. Now, Clark's parents visited for the holidays, but their visits never had quite the same presence for Billy, and Crystal missed her own grandparents too much to cultivate it on his behalf. The room wasn't even prepared for her in-laws, and when Billy had asked about gathering supplies to work on crafts with his grandmother, Crystal had worried about the extra mess. The sharp sting of guilt and regret sliced in Crystal's nose as she sniffled back a sob.

Besides her grandparents' annual visit, the tree itself was what she had loved the most about the holiday, Crystal reflected, coming to pause beneath a towering oak tree. Edged in silver frost, it glittered blue in the moonlight as if someone had wrapped a strand of pale lights through its branches. Crystal slipped off one of her gloves and traced her fingers along the edges of the bottlebrush branch. Her fingers were nearly the same shade of eerie blue as the frost on the tips of the green tendrils, but she paid this no mind as her thoughts trekked backward once more.

Selecting the Christmas tree had been her family's most sacred ritual—and one that demanded a good portion of the year in observance. In August, she and her parents would travel to a little-known tree farm not far from their home. They would spend all day wandering through the fields until they'd selected the perfect tree, which would be bound by a ribbon bearing their name until they could return after Thanksgiving. Those tree days were long and glorious, and Crystal would spend the majority of her time running around the forest of domesticated trees in neat rows, wandering as far out as she could without getting in trouble. In December, she'd help her dad saw it down and tie it to the roof of their car. When they got it home, the ritual involved pushing all of the living room furniture out of the way and covering the floor in newspaper, because of course, the tree they'd chosen would be too big and in need of pre-stand modifications. The rest of the evening would be spent cutting some off the trunk or clipping various branches in order to make it fit. The house would be scented with the tang of pine, and her mother would brew hot cider laden with cinnamon sticks to toast the arrival of the tree.

Crystal sucked back another sob and wandered through the wild forest. She and Clark had taken Billy to purchase a tree from a pre-cut lot this year. She'd wanted a plastic tree, but Billy had balked, and the short little pine had been her compromise, though it had already begun to drop its needles. Crystal brushed the ice from her fingertips and returned her frozen fingers into her glove, hiding them away as if the gloves could conceal her shame at reducing such a beloved ritual into a mundane, selfish chore. She was too cold now to even notice that her movements had grown stiff and uncoordinated, or that she could no longer feel the sting of tears on her cheeks.

Standing half-frozen in the cold and quiet and lacking the energy to keep walking, Crystal realized it wasn't just the warmth of decorations and family that she had lost, but the spirit of the season itself, and she wasn't sure when it had left her. It had happened so gradually and so subtly that Crystal couldn't point to a moment when, like the Grinch, her heart had shrunk three sizes too small and she'd gone from loving every second of the season to dreading its arrival. But now, here she was, and the space between the girl she had been and the coldhearted woman she had become was so striking and vast that it was almost impossible to believe and even harder to accept. She'd continued to go through the motions, but along the way she had lost her joy. Now she was just icy, an inflexible version of the girl she had been—hard and cold like a fossil retrieved from layers of ice. Iced over like the rose bushes in her backyard.

Crystal heard the metallic jingling noise again. This time it wasn't the sound of bells that it had been before, but a faint clang—the sound of metal on metal somewhere in the distance. She turned her head and listened, holding her breath. A thin wind picked up, a woodland flow of passionate air, and bushy evergreen branches susurrated in response. Another clang sounded, spurring her into action.

"Hello," she called into the dark night. "Is anyone there?"

No voice returned her call, but after a moment another ring of metal sounded in the air.

Crystal pushed away from the tree, moving sluggishly through the snow. She looked up toward the western horizon and saw the moon blurred and haloed behind a high veil of cirrostratus nebulosus. The snow was falling heavier now, so thickly that even the trees in front of her were obscured by the curtain of its fall. Crystal waved her hand in front of her, calling again. "Hello, is anyone there? Can you hear me?"

The sound did not repeat itself. Crystal began to wonder if she had even heard it. Perhaps it had been nothing but the wind.

AS CRYSTAL STOMPED DEEPER INTO THE WOODS AND SNOW, SHE eventually heard the clang again, and she whirled around to the direction she thought it came from. It was a foreign sound, unfitting to the land. The first could be dismissed as tinnitus, the second as the trilling of birds, maybe, or the sound of wind whistling through frozen branches, but hearing it again Crystal knew that the noise was nothing so simple as that. It wasn't the jingling of bells as she'd first thought, but it was metal—tempered steel against steel.

Ahead of her lay a field of white, unbroken by trees for

some distance, ending in a line of evergreens as if artificially demarcated. The distant wall was a black silhouette rising from refracted snow-shine, reaching with slightly swaying points tapering into the night. Crystal trudged through the snow toward the trees, hoping to hear the sound again. The score of hollow wind, rueful and underlaid with a whine, dominated the soundscape. It picked up grains of snow and threw them against her face. As Crystal approached, she found the trees more spread out than they had appeared, allowing her to penetrate the thicket with ease. Deep inside, she stopped. She turned in a slow circle, curtailing her breath, and trying to pick up any sound that could transcend the sough of the wind.

There it was again. A clear clang, then a *shiiiiing*. It was louder than before. She was close. Seconds later, another metallic sound pierced the air, and Crystal scrambled eagerly in its direction. As she advanced, the sound became more steady, though its tones changed. It was soft and then hard, fast and slow, irregular, alternating at intervals spaced apart by several breaths.

Someone was fighting. It sounded like swords.

Unsure of what she might be walking into, Crystal decided to walk more cautiously, which was challenging now since her legs were so stiff she could barely lift her knees high enough to clear the snow with each footfall. It was unbelievable that anyone would be out here, especially someone sword fighting. Part of her wanted to go back the way she had come, but there was nothing to return to. So she pushed through the brush, looking each way, trying to suss out the sound's direction. Searching for a visual clue, she noticed a lighter shade of night in one direction. No, not saw it—not exactly. It was more a feeling than a visual, and Crystal nonetheless aimed herself in its direction.

As she made her way toward the noise, the wind picked up, snatching loose snow from the branches around her and tossing them defiantly in her face. The pale, icy moon had turned to a shimmering shade of glacier blue, and branches scraped at her collar without being pushed away first, leaving snow to accumulate at weak points in her clothing. She felt heavy, like her body was soaking and swelling with the ice and snow, hardening like clay in a frozen forest kiln.

But the sound of battle was clear, and it was just ahead, behind a veil of trees silhouetted sharply against a light sparking in the darkness. It filled the clearing ahead of her with a pulsing violet hue, something dreamlike and surreal. A sense of foreboding came over her, but an undeniable curiosity came with it, and Crystal was overcome with the feeling that she was meant to see this. She pressed on determinedly, hoping that whoever was making the noise might also have something to warm her. An old song came into her thoughts, a familiar old carol she'd heard once on the radio, but the words seemed different now—more full of meaning than they'd ever been before:

Then rang the bells more loud and deep, God is not dead, nor does he sleep

CRYSTAL CAME TO THE LAST LAYER OF TREES THAT INEFFECTIVELY imprisoned the light, and the brightness beyond was blinding. It was unnatural, stark against the dark that surrounded it. It didn't flicker and undulate, but it was warm and welcoming. Looking behind her, Crystal now saw nothing but black. It was as if the world beyond this place—beyond this moment—had ceased to exist, fading away like a dream behind her. Another jarring clang resounded, followed by scraping metal and lesser clangs.

And then there was silence.

The wind seemed to stop. Snowflakes fell in slow motion. Even the clangs fell suddenly silent. Crystal could hear her breath. Fear washed over her for the first time since she'd awoken in her car. She was terrified. She could see nothing through the trees, just purplish-white light spilling out between them and their branches, doing nothing to light the world beyond. Even the moon and stars had disappeared into a cloudless purple sky. There was no longer anything else but this place. It wasn't even cold anymore—no, it was cold, but Crystal had ceased to feel it. She lifted a gloved finger to her face and touched her cheek, shocked when it felt solid and hard beneath her hand.

Her heart pounding, Crystal reached between two trees with one arm and drew back some branches, holding her hand in front of her to shield her eyes from the brightness. She could see a circular field surrounded by a ring of trees—a forest fairy ring. There was fog in the air, giving the land a hazy appearance. And then she saw *them*.

If her throat had been thawed enough to scream, Crystal's voice would have ripped forth to shatter the silence of the night. But the cold had sealed her lips and she could do little more than suck air inside her mouth as she saw the creatures awaiting her inside the clearing.

THERE WERE TWO MEN, BOTH WIELDING SWORDS LONGER THAN ANY Crystal had ever seen. No, she decided, when her mind had had time to process the image before her. They were, in fact, not men at all, but things that only resembled the shape of men. They were giants—that much was clear—and they had bodies made of torsos and arms and legs, but they were not human.

They looked more like trees come to life, as if two of the mighty evergreens in the forest had shaken off their snowy limbs, twisted loose a sliver of stone, and marched into battle. Both were tall and proud, with limbs formed of thick branches, and carved wooden faces from which sprouted curling beards of foliage and flowers with colors bright against the snowy backdrop. Large and lumbering, the beings nonetheless moved with an unwieldy grace, as if their movements were an act of nature itself and not the calculated gestures of any more mundane living creature. The two giants of green faced each other, swords in twiggy hands, locked in a battle for domination. One seemed more plant than man, the other more man than plant.

Of the two beings before her, one was much smaller than the other. He seemed a shriveled and nearly dead thing, his body misshapen and constructed of the twisted bark of decaying oak tree. His form was clothed in leaves that had largely faded from green into the waning hues of fall—flimsy, tissue-paper scraps of yellow and crimson and brown that rustled against the curling narrow roots that edged his form as he moved, falling under and narrowly missing the slicing sword of his opponent. Around this giant's head was wound a crown of acorns, and even now the small ovals loosened from their hold and tumbled to the snow at his feet as the woodland King of Oak collapsed onto his knees.

Standing over him, the other giant was more grand and robust, a figure assembled as much by pine as by frost itself so that he was a hulking, vibrant thing in comparison to the King of Oak, who was now struggling back onto his feet. The green of this larger giant's body was bright and pulsing, decorated with glistening holly berries that shone like drops of blood against snow, and he wore a crown of horn braided with glistening, silver-tipped holly atop his head so that he looked like a great stag as he dashed across the snow, stabbing at his foe.

Crystal watched in amazement as the two men—the two winter gods with crowns of oak and holly—battled tirelessly, the King of Oak waning but refusing to surrender against the might of the King of Holly. She lost all sense of time as she took in their fierce battle, too immersed in the spectacular beauty of the fight to even wince when their swords shrieked in the frozen air.

It seemed the battle would last forever until, finally, exhausted and broken, the King of Holly collapsed onto all fours, his body heaving with breath. The King of Oak walked beside his enemy's head, angled himself, and swung his sword up and back with both hands, arching it behind him. He held that position for only a moment before releasing a guttural shout that rent the air and swinging the sword down with tensed muscles and a cry of victory. The blade swang true and the edge cut through flesh with a sound of thick wetness. The head dropped with a thud into the snow and rolled from the body, spotting the snow with blood, and the rest of the man of holly and pine slumped forward as his arms gave out, collapsing over the sword as his crown tumbled into the snow beside him. Blood pooled and the forest once again fell silent.

The King of Oak stayed in his doubled-over position, hands still on the hilt of his sword and face pointed down, as if out of respect for his adversary or perhaps in grief. He then slowly raised himself upright, loosing his sword from the slain body of the fallen king as he stood tall, arms lank to either side. The dead leaves of his armor rustled in a lazy breeze and even as Crystal stared at them their colors appeared to change, their dusty fall colors sharpening into brilliance, and the brittle bark of his roots growing thicker. The crown atop his head became immediately fuller, sprouting new growth to replace what had fallen before, and by the time this was all done the King of Oak seemed renewed, as if the life he had taken had rekindled in him, and Crystal watched as the ruined body of the King of Holly grew pale and withered in the snow.

Suddenly, Crystal realized the King of Oak's pupil-less eyes were staring at her.

The fear that had eased within Crystal reignited, the sudden surge as sharp and numbing as frostbite, as a frigid stiffness overcame Crystal where she stood at the edge of the ring. The bright purple hue of the light dimmed as darkness crept in at the edges of her vision, her eyes growing as mullioned as the windows of her car when she'd woken in the snow bank. The wind faded and died, the flecks of snow suspending in mid-fall in the air before her as the King of Oak stepped closer, his leaves adding rustling murmurs to the air around him as he pushed through the small barrier of branches that guarded the entrance to the fairy ring.

The king's presence was more an awareness than a physical sensation. She could no longer feel anything, she discovered. Her body was locked in place, too cold and frozen to even twitch her fingers, and when the King of Oak's eyes found hers, an icy blast funneled through her, rooting her to the ground where she stood as if she were a tree herself. She found that she could barely move her lips, but she managed to whisper a few words, her voice as crisp and fragile as glass. "What *is* this?"

The King of Oak replied with a godlike voice, deep and imposing. "Fear not, my child. Neither of us truly dies. My brother here will be born again on the other side of the year."

The silence that followed was jarring. The reverberations of his voice lingered. The King of Oak held his stoic gaze. Moments passed. Then he continued, waving his branch-like arm behind him. "He lives on even now, see?"

Crystal glimpsed movement. The King of Holly stepped out from behind his brother and took up an equally imposing stare. Crystal looked down and noticed his body was gone from where it had lain before. The dark spots of blood in the snow, black in the blue light, were gone. The head was back on his shoulders. He was reassembled in all his former glory—all holly and horn and ivy—though he looked diminished somehow, as if he was fighting a long-awaited sleep.

The King of Oak went on. "My brother's power continues its reign through the winter"—he gestured with his hand to the King of Holly—"though it wanes as mine grows, until he fades with the coming summer. I shall yield to him in the same fashion come the waning of the year. It is the cycle of things, the rhythm of the season that moves from dark to light, warmth to winter."

The king's speech was lucid and sonorous, followed by a period of silence that signified a finality to the oration. Crystal waited for him to say more, but he didn't, and as she watched, the two figures began to grow hazy in her vision as ice crystals formed over her eyes. Her body was no longer able to move, and when her gaze flicked to her hand, she saw that her glove was gone. In its place was the shape of her hand, no longer a living, fleshy thing but a form carved from ice. She was becoming frozen after all.

Gasping, Crystal managed to usher a few more brittle words through her painfully frozen lips. "What is happening to me?"

"You have lost sight of what it means to die and be

reborn," the kings continued, speaking in unison now so that their voices collided in a thundering tenor that shook the snow from the nearest branches. "You have become as cold as the winter itself, rigid and unforgiving, forsaking the warmth that would rekindle your spirit like my brother's blood rekindles the earth. You have chosen to isolate yourself in the trimmings of a manmade holiday, and you have clung to your coldness rather than anticipate the return of the light. Your family waits for you with love and memories while you worry about things that don't matter and waste your time, turning your eyes away from the brightest moments in this darkest time of year."

Crystal tried to speak again, but ice had sealed her lips.

"Your coldness has hardened you," spoke the King of Holly. "Left unchanged, a heart so cold must stay in winter with me, for it has no place in the warmth of light that now returns to the land under my brother's reign."

No, please, Crystal pleaded, though she could no longer speak. *I want to change. I don't want to freeze.*

But the kings did not hear her. Instead, they offered one final cryptic statement. "Like the day itself, there is always darkness before the light, Crystal Townsend. Find the fire within yourself or your heart will forever be as cold as ice."

With a solemn bow, both giants dissolved as the darkness crept into Crystal's vision. She was suddenly completely alone in the frozen forest, and the last sound Crystal heard was that of her own breath as it caught in her throat—two stuttering, rasping final breaths before the icy chill in her veins hardened and she could no longer breathe. As the last bit of air remaining in her lungs escaped her, she watched as her frozen, ice-sculpture hand turned translucent and hung like five pointed icicles on the branch she'd been grasping. A terrible, freezing stiffness overcame her as her vision turned blue, then purple, and then faded to nothingness.

CRYSTAL OPENED HER EYES.

It was warm where she was—warm and soft, and so un-like the dark, frozen forest where she'd seen the two old kings battle for midwinter.

She blinked, and as her vision finally cleared she realized she was in her bedroom, tucked beneath the heavy blankets of her bed. The room was filled with the early gray light of predawn, and the clock on her bedside table read seven a.m.

Beside her, the space where Clark normally slept was emp-ty, but there was still a dent in the pillow where his head had lain while he slept. Crystal rolled into Clark's empty trench and the sheets were cool, not cold, as if he hadn't been gone long. She inhaled and could still smell her husband's scent on the green flannel sheets that he always insisted be put on the bed for the month of December. Normally she thought the sheets were tacky and impractical, but this morning there was something very alive and comforting about them.

They reminded her of the King of Holly's bristling ivy ar-mor, and the King of Oak's words came back to her: "There is always darkness before the light, Crystal Townsend. Find the fire within yourself or your heart will forever be as cold as ice."

Sitting upright, Crystal checked that her fingers were hers as she remembered them—thin and fair—and not the frozen stalagmites they'd become in her dream, if that was what it had been. Finding them whole, she pushed the blankets away from her and swung her feet out of her bed. She slipped her arms inside her robe and pounded down the stairs into her living room, not daring to breathe again until her eyes found Clark and Billy, both sipping cocoa where they sat on the couch, watching an animated holiday cartoon.

"Oh, hey," Clark said, twisting his head over his shoulder to smile at his wife. "Sleep well?"

Crystal shook her head as she sank into the seat beside her son, gathering his small body up into her arms. "I'm not sure," she admitted. She inhaled deeply, nestling her nose in the fuzzy down of her son's hair. He smelled warm, like cookies pulled fresh from the oven, and so full of life.

"It's still the Texas Ice Age outside," Clark continued, and the words sounded familiar to Crystal's ears. She looked through the window and stared at the white flecks sprinkling down from the sky.

"Snowmaggedon," she answered before she could stop herself. "The battle for midwinter."

Clark laughed and noisily sipped from his mug. "Well, today is the winter solstice," he agreed before asking, "So what errands are on your list today?"

Crystal tightened her grip on Billy, watching the snow as it fell outside. She remembered the ice on her hands and the frost in her throat, the way the King of Oak's eyes had sent that debilitating coldness through to her heart when he'd looked into hers. She thought of being alone and cold and frightened in the forest, and for the first time in a long time, the weather outside looked suddenly beautiful as she snuggled her son and reached over to brush a stray strand of Clark's hair behind his ear. "Nothing," she said at last. "Absolutely nothing."

ABOUT THE AUTHORS

Sam Hooker

Sam writes darkly humorous fantasy novels about thing like tyrannical despots and the masked scoundrels who tickle them without mercy. He knows all the best swear words, though he refuses to repeat them because he doesn't want to attract goblins.

Alcy Leyva

Alcy Leyva is a Bronx-born writer, teacher, and pizza enthusiast. He graduated from Hunter College with a B.A. in English (Creative Writing) and an MFA in Fiction from The New School. He has been published in Popmatters, The Rumpus, Entropy Mag, and Quiet Lunch Magazine.

Laura Morrison

Laura Morrison lives in the Metro Detroit area. She has a B.S. in applied ecology and environmental science from Michigan Technological University. Before she was a writer and stay-at-home mom, she battled invasive species and researched turtles.

Cassondra Windwalker

Cassondra Windwalker is a poet and novelist writing full time from the coast of the Kenai Peninsula in Alaska. She is supported by a tolerant husband, three wandering offspring, a useless dog, and a zombie cat. Her hobbies include hiking, photography, and having other people's demons over for tea.

Dalena Storm

Dalena Storm has lived in India, Japan, Germany, and on both coasts of the United States. She currently resides in a converted general store in the woods of Western Massachusetts with a rare Burmese temple cat, a purring black fluffbeast, a professor of magic, and an infant with an astonishing ability to resist sleep.

Seven Jane

Seven Jane is a bestselling author of dark fantasy and speculative fiction. Seven is a member of The Author's Guild and Women's Fiction Writing Association. She also writes a column for The Women's Fiction Association and is a contributor to The Nerd Daily.

ACKNOWLEDGEMENTS

I'd like to acknowledge my husband, Jason Storm, for his sharp editorial eye and helpful imaginings as I created this story. Moreover, I'd like to thank him for building a life with me, complete with its own traditions and magical rituals that make the world brighter during the long, cold winter.

- Dalena Storm

Many thanks to the lovely and mysterious Stanley Hotel and the town of Estes Park, of my favorite places in Colorado. All naccuracies are creative liberties.

- Cassondra Windwalker

M, for providing the inspiration for this story. And to Liz, making sure "goulash" didn't go to print, and pointing that most people are familiar with the evils of glitter.

- Seven Jane

d from all the authors to Lynn Shaw, for everything.

31901065467286